"Stay here with me until bedtime."

Miranda's words made Adam look down at her in surprise. It was the first time she had ever tried to detain him.

"I'm afraid you must find the evenings dull," he said.

"No, no, the others I do not mind, but tonight is different. You are different."

"Am I?" He stood regarding her with an odd expression. "Is it possible you are trying to flirt with me, Miranda?" he asked.

She looked up at him. "Yes," she replied with firmness.

His eyebrows lifted. "That might be dangerous in the circumstances," he said softly. "I'm flesh and blood, you know, in spite of our platonic agreement."

"Our agreement was of your making," she replied, the heavy lashes veiling her eyes.

Great love stories never grow old...

And we at Harlequin are proud to welcome you to
HARLEQUIN CLASSIC LIBRARY—a prime selection
of time-tested, enduring favorites from the early lists
of Harlequin's best-selling Romances.

Harlequin Romances have been read throughout the
world for many years. Why? There are as many reasons
as there are people. But longtime readers tell us that our
books combine the enjoyment of travel, the intrigue of
good plots, warm and interesting characters and the
thrill of love. Each novel possesses an emotional appeal
that sweeps you right into the wonderful world of
romance!

As publishers of Harlequin Romances, we take a great
deal of pride in our books. Since 1949 Harlequin has
built its reputation on the solid base of quality and
originality. And now our widely popular paperback
romance novels have been translated into eighteen
languages and are sold in more than eighty countries.

So... if you relish a classic love story, one whose appeal
has lost nothing over the years, read these timeless
romances in the HARLEQUIN CLASSIC LIBRARY.
We hope you enjoy this story and all the others in
our special selection of beautiful love stories from
years past.

For a free catalogue of the books available, write to:
HARLEQUIN READER SERVICE
(In the U.S.) M.P.O. Box 707, Niagara Falls, N.Y. 14302
(In Canada) Stratford, Ontario, Canada   N5A 6W2

Wintersbride

SARA SEALE

Originally published as Harlequin Romance #560

HARLEQUIN
CLASSIC LIBRARY

TORONTO·LONDON·NEW YORK·AMSTERDAM
SYDNEY·HAMBURG·PARIS·STOCKHOLM

Original hardcover edition published by
Mills & Boon Limited 1951
ISBN 0-373-80018-5

Harlequin edition first published January 1961
Golden Harlequin Library edition, Volume XXIV,
published March 1972
Harlequin Classic Library edition published April 1980

Printed in Canada

CHAPTER ONE

ADAM CHANTRY DID not know why the fair should attract him. It was a shoddy little collection of booths and amusement stalls erected temporarily on a piece of waste ground at the end of the promenade. A sad, dirty little fair that repelled rather than invited patronage.

Adam had walked along the front after an indifferent dinner at his hotel, cursing the late consultation at the hospital that had necessitated his staying the night. His thoughts turned homeward to Wintersbride and the daughter he knew so little. Fay would be in bed now, perhaps asleep, perhaps in one of her imperious moods with the watchful Simmy warding off a scene with her accustomed astuteness. Thank heaven for Simmy, Adam thought rather wearily. He sighed sharply. His friends were right, he supposed; he should marry again. And he thought of Grace who had so deeply admired the dead Melisande and who was waiting humbly yet confidently to step into her shoes.

He frowned as he walked, so that people glanced at him speculatively, wondering who he was with his faint air of distinction and dark, impatient face. But Grace—no. He could not bear to live with an echo of Melisande's early perfection. They were too alike, she and Melisande, and he wanted no more of women now, least of all the gentle but still demanding devotion that Grace was so ready to give him. His work had been all-sufficing for years, and only lately had he come to realize that his daughter perhaps needed something more than his own and Simmy's careful vigilance. She would look at him with hostile eyes, summing him up with that precocious maturity that was so disturbing, withdrawing from him into her own small, self-centered world.

It was at this point in his reflections that he became aware of the fair. It was nearly dark but still too early to turn back to the hotel and go to bed. His thoughts were unpleasant company this evening, and he decided to seek a brief diversion in what attractions the fair had to offer. They were not many.

He passed the tent that housed the two-headed calf, having no liking for monstrosities, paused for a moment to watch the hula girls waggling their hips invitingly and found that in the next booth the knife thrower had already closed down for the night. There remained only the tent of the Mighty Mesmero, whose garish poster claimed him to be The Greatest Hypnotist in All Europe.

"Mesmero and Tojo are unique in show business," a man in a purple sweater was shouting from the little platform. "This young boy whom I will now show you was found on the steppes of Asia by the maestro, who ever since has exercised a remarkable control over him. He is both deaf and dumb and his actions are entirely governed by the Mighty Mesmero's unique powers. Tojo—come show yourself."

Adam's mouth gave a small skeptical quirk. He had yet to see the act in which genuine hypnotism was performed. The boy was climbing onto the platform, stumbling a little as he mounted the rickety steps. He was dressed in the conventional Eastern tight trousers and tunic, with tarnished costume jewelery, but the turban had been replaced by a tight spangled skullcap that gave him the illusion of a sad harlequin. Adam was about to turn away when something in the boy's expression made him frown and observe him with a more professional eye. Was it possible that this was the authentic thing after all? The boy stood there, his eyes wide and unblinking in the naphtha flares, looking straight over the heads of the small crowd. He swayed a little as he stood, and that blank, fixed gaze never wavered.

"Deaf and dumb," the showman was repeating. "Completely dependent on the Mighty Mesmero for all his actions—even his very thoughts. You will see, ladies and gentlemen, the most remarkable demonstration . . . ."

The man's voice went on monotonously, delivering his patter, but Adam was not listening. The Mighty Mesmero in flowing robes now appeared on the platform. He was unimpressive and Adam doubted if he could hypnotize a fly. Beside his coarse features the boy's face took on a startling look of delicacy, and he edged slightly away. Mesmero made some ineffectual gestures to the audience, then disappeared again into the tent, pushing the boy before him. Adam paid his sixpence and joined the the small knot of people who followed them.

The tent was dark and stuffy and there was the heavy scent of incense burning somewhere.

Behind the scenes someone started up a gramophone, and to the jarring strains of a well-worn record of Eastern music, the curtain was drawn jerkily aside.

The boy sat in a high-backed chair on a raised dais looking straight ahead. Mesmero moved slowly toward the dais, his hands outstretched in the conventional gesture of casting a spell.

"I will now put this boy into a state of trance and he will be submissive to my will," he said in a sonorous broken accent. "Tojo—look at me." The boy slowly turned his head. "Look in my eyes . . . submit . . . submit. . . ."

The boy swallowed convulsively, then said quite clearly, "I cannot. . . ."

Someone tittered and murmured audibly, "Deaf and dumb, I don't think!"

"Tojo!" Mesmero thundered. "You will obey!"

"I—I cannot," the boy said again, and slumped forward in his chair.

For a moment Mesmero stood uncertainly; then he announced solemnly to the skeptical audience, "Silence! Tojo is in trance."

"You'd better stop this nonsense, the boy's ill," Adam said quietly, and pushed his way through the little group of people. The man in the purple sweater appeared suddenly from outside and began to clear the tent.

"Who are you?" Mesmero asked imperiously, but he looked frightened.

"I'm a doctor," Adam replied, and bent over the boy.

Now he knew what had puzzled him about him. Even when he had been standing outside on the platform he had been on the verge of collapse. Adam lifted him out of the chair and, laying him flat on the grass, loosened his tunic and felt for his heart. He looked up quickly with a sardonic lift of the eyebrows.

"You're a phony all through, aren't you, Mesmero?" he remarked. "Why trouble to hide her sex? Isn't a girl a more glamorous addition to an act than a boy?"

Mesmero looked uneasy.

"It has always been so. The Mighty Mesmero and Tojo. We are known everywhere in show business, and we cannot change the act because the real boy is missing. I know nothing about this girl, doctor. She comes to me, she wants a job, the show opens in half an hour and there is no Tojo. I look at her, she is small, thin, she will pass for a boy. What could I do?"

"There's no law as far as I know against girls impersonating boys on the stage or vice versa," retorted Adam. "Cut short the protestations and fetch me some water."

THE GIRL opened her eyes. They were gray and heavily lashed and looked too big for her thin, delicate face.

"Who are you?" she asked.

"I'm a doctor," Adam said. "You fainted at the beginning of your act. Lie still, you'll feel better soon."

She pulled off the tight skullcap with a sigh of relief. Without it she looked less strained and pinched, though the impression of delicacy was heightened. Her hair, so fair that it was silver rather than gold, was cut short and curled over her head like a very young child's.

Adam smiled involuntarily.

"How did you come to get mixed up with a bunch like this?" he asked. "You don't belong among these people."

"I do not belong anywhere," she replied sedately. "But I have to eat."

Mesmero came back with a glass of water and she took it from him, gravely sipping it.

"I'm afraid I spoiled your act, Mr. Mesmero," she said. "You should have let me have that meal when I asked you for it."

"There was no time," he blustered. "You had to be rehearsed, you had to get dressed. There was one little half hour and you had to think of food!"

"Have you ever been hungry, Mr. Mesmero?" she said gently, and Adam glanced at her sharply.

"When did you last have a proper meal?" he asked.

"Two days ago—I think," she replied. "You see, I had to pay for my room, and I could not have a room and eat, as well."

"You did not tell me this. I know nothing about you," Mesmero protested. "But now I pay you for the performance you ruined and you go and get a meal. That is generous, *hein*?"

"But you said I could stay here until the fair moved on."

"No, no, no, that is impossible. There is no room."

The strange little air of composure left her and her face crumpled up like a child's.

"But I have nowhere to go," she said.

"What about this room that took all the money you should have spent on food?" Adam inquired with skeptical amusement.

"My landlady let my room this morning. I could not have afforded to stay on without a job anyway," she said, and the uncontrollable tears of the result of overstrain filled her eyes.

Adam made a quick decision. She was nearer a breakdown than he had at first supposed. The whole situation was bizarre and possibly quite spurious, but professional instinct would not allow him to abandon her in such circumstances.

"You had better come back with me to my hotel and they'll find you a room for the night," he said prosaically. "I have to return to my home tomorrow, but in the morning we can talk."

She looked at him suspiciously.

"But I don't know you," she said with sudden primness.

His smile was a little sardonic.

"What difference does that make? You didn't know the Mighty Mesmero, either, but you were prepared to spend the night here."

He had deliberately spoken sharply and he saw her flush.

"That was different," she replied. "It was a business proposition."

"Well, we can't discuss business at this hour and place. Look on me as a meal ticket if you like, but come along."

"Yes, yes, go with the gentleman," said Mesmero hastily. "The fair is closing down and we do not want the police inquiring why we do not close the booths."

"Or one or two other little things, I shouldn't be surprised," said Adam pleasantly.

The man gave him a quick, suspicious look, then hustled the girl out of the tent to the caravan where she had changed her clothes.

Adam had managed to get hold of a taxi while he was waiting, for he did not think she was fit to walk back to the hotel. He glanced at her with mild curiosity as she walked across the grass from the caravan, carrying a small suitcase, but her age still defeated him.

"Feeling better?" he asked.

"Empty," she said as he took the suitcase from her.

"Well, we'll soon remedy that. Come along."

As the car drew up at the hotel, he said, "By the way, what's your name?"

"Miranda," she replied. "Miranda Clare."

Most of the residents had gone to bed, for it was nearly eleven o'clock.

"The young lady will be staying the night if you have a room. A patient of mine," Adam said to the sleepy reception clerk.

"Certainly, Mr. Chantry," the man replied. "On the same floor as yours?"

"It doesn't matter," Adam said indifferently, and caught a wide grin on the girl's face. It changed her completely, lending her an air of mischief that was very charming. His answering glance was severe and he turned to the clerk.

"Can the kitchen produce a meal of sorts?" he asked, frowning.

"I'll see what I can do, sir," the man said. "For one—upstairs?"

"For one—in the dining room."

He took the girl into a small smoking room that was deserted. The remains of a fire burned in the grate. Miranda crouched beside it and held out her cold, slender hands to the warmth.

"The clerk thinks you have improper designs on me," she said. "Have you?"

"My dear child!" He was beginning to feel annoyed. "You are very clearly young enough to be my daughter."

"Why, how old are you?" she asked him gravely.

"Thirty-eight."

"You would have to have been rather precocious to be my father," she said with a little smile. "I'm nineteen."

"Then you ought to know better than to join up with a ruffian like the Mighty Mesmero." He sounded brusque. "I suppose you realize what would have been the end of it?"

"I suppose so. But when one is hungry and without any money, one does not stop to think. You haven't a very good bedside manner, have you?" she said.

"I don't need a bedside manner in my profession."

"I thought you said you were a doctor. You aren't, are you? The clerk addressed you as mister."

"I'm a surgeon, not a general practitioner. My dear girl, what do you really suppose I've brought you here for?"

"I don't know. As I said before, when you're hungry and without a lodging you do not ask too many questions."

He moved impatiently. He could not make her out. One moment she was like the child he had first taken her for, the next she was discussing very adult problems with a provocative air of composure.

"And are you prepared then to—shall we say, humor me—for the price of a night's lodging and comfort?" he asked.

She looked across at him, seeing the sudden hardness in his

dark face, the indifferent coolness in his eyes, and the hands she was holding to the fire suddenly trembled.

"I—I don't think my ideas are very coherent," she faltered.

She had gone very white, and before he could speak again she broke into a storm of weeping.

"Now, look here, this won't do," he said, and his voice was suddenly gentle. "You were pulling my leg, weren't you, and perhaps I was pulling yours? You may be nineteen and highly versed in the ways of the world, but at the moment you're nothing but an overwrought child and I should know better than to permit scenes of this kind. Now, stop crying, and tell me how you've come to be landed in such a predicament."

Weeping, she told him her story. There was little to relate. She had spent much of her life in France with an artist father. She had no mother. Someone called Pierre Morel figured in the story, but whether he was a brother or a friend, Adam could not gather. A year ago, her father had crossed to England without her. He had been failing in health for some time, but how ill he was no one had guessed. He had been carried off the boat in a critical condition and taken straight to hospital, where he had died in the operating room. It had taken some time for the authorities to trace her, and by the time the news reached France, Frank Clare had been buried for a week.

"Who is this Pierre?" asked Adam. "Didn't he look after you when your father died, as there seems to be no one else?"

"He did what he could, but he had no money, either, and his affairs were in a delicate state, you understand? He could not show me too much attention because of the Latours."

"Who are the Latours?"

"Distant cousins of his."

"Then he's not a relative of yours?"

"Pierre? Oh, no, no, but a very dear friend. Pierre is French. He used to tease me and say he would marry me when I grew up, but I think by now he is married to Marguerite Latour, because of the money, you see."

"And then you came to England?" he prompted.

"Yes. Pierre remembered my mother had relatives in England, but when I got here I found they had gone overseas many years ago. There was no means of tracing them. Pierre sent me a little money, but he could not afford much, and I could not go back to France—to Pierre. It would have upset the Latours, which was only natural. When he and Marguerite married, he said, they would have me to stay and find me a husband in the French fashion."

"But you are not French, Miranda." said Adam a little dryly. "Wouldn't you mind being married off in the French fashion, as you call it?"

"No," she said. "Security is better than independence, and I am not romantic."

"You won't always feel like that. You're very young."

She had stopped crying and now she looked at him with an air of tolerant wisdom that he found rather disconcerting.

"No, my friend," she said. "After a year of accepting any job that would keep me alive, I shall never scoff at security. If you must have love thrown in, well—I do not think it would be difficult to make yourself love someone who was reasonably decent."

His eyebrows went up, but all he said was, "You have some rather startling ideas. Ah, here's your supper."

While she ate she told Adam something about the way she had been living for the past year. She was skilled at nothing useful, she said, and she had no references. She was too young, too old, too talkative, too silent, and always she was inexperienced.

"Whatever the job, I was wrong," she said. By the time she had chanced on the fair and the Mighty Mesmero, she was hungry and homeless and without a penny.

"If I had not been starving I would have enjoyed it," she said. "It's all trickery, you know. He could not have hypnotized me, really."

"Enjoyed it?" he sounded skeptical.

She frowned.

"Well, no, perhaps not. I hate being stared at. But if I had not been hungry and the tent so stuffy, I wouldn't have fainted and spoiled the act and I might have got around Mr. Mesmero to let me stay with them when the fair moved on.''

"I've no doubt you would," remarked Adam dryly. "And duly regretted it, I fear, when the Mighty Mesmero began to get fresh.''

She lowered her heavy lashes.

"Yes, well—as I said, I did not think of that at the time. The sort of men *I've* run across were fond of curves—"she sketched a vague outline with her lively hands "—and people are apt to think me much younger than I am. It's an advantage, you know, except when you're dealing with prospective employers.''

She carefully scraped the last vestige of food from her plate, then leaned back in her chair with a sigh of repletion.

"That was the most wonderful meal I've ever eaten,'' she said. She closed her eyes, and Adam saw the blue transparency of her eyelids and the deep smudges that lay below.

For a moment he experienced a tenderness toward her that he had not known for any human being for many years, the tenderness he could perhaps have felt for his daughter, had she ever wanted it.

"Come along before you drop off to sleep,'' he said, getting to his feet abruptly. "We'll go and find out what room they've given you, and tomorrow we must decide what's to be done with you.''

He himself did not sleep well and by the time he was called he was already regretting his impulse of the night before. What on earth was he going to do with this unexpected scrap of humanity? He could hardly go back to Devonshire and leave her stranded in this strange town without even the price of her next night's lodging.

He went down to breakfast in a bad mood and was relieved to find that Miranda did not join him. There was a letter for him from Grace and he frowned at it, wondering irritably why she always found it necessary to write to him the minute he was away from home. There was already more than a proprietary hint in the flowing, well-turned sentences, and Adam realized with a small sense of shock that not only Grace and her mother, but most of their friends, were expecting him to marry her. He thrust the letter into his pocket and told himself angrily that he had never given her the slightest encouragement. She had been Melisande's friend and later it had seemed only natural that she should take an interest in Melisande's motherless child. He had been grateful to her and had valued her help in the difficult months after his wife's tragic death, and later when friends began to hint that he should marry again, he had found her a protection against the obvious machinations of other mothers of eligible daughters. He had supposed, a little wryly, that even a not-so-young widower with a difficult daughter was made attractive by wealth and a brilliant reputation, for he ranked high in his profession and made a great deal of money.

He did not believe that Grace was in love with him, but she was over thirty and wanted marriage and a position.

With a quick, irritable stride, he left the dining room and went upstairs to see Miranda.

She was sitting up in bed, a breakfast tray across her knees. Already, he thought, she looked better, although he now saw that she was painfully thin.

"Good morning," she said with her mouth full, "I hope you did not mind, but breakfast in bed is such a luxury. Besides, it is better for your reputation, do you not think?"

He frowned.

"What's my reputation got to do with it?"

"Well, suddenly appearing at breakfast in public with a strange girl—people might think things."

This aspect of the affair had not occurred to him, but seeing her wide eyes fixed on him unblinkingly, he was not altogether sure that regard for his reputation would greatly worry her.

"Well, now, what are we going to do with you?" he said briskly. "You need rest, you know, and a certain amount of building up before you tackle any more jobs. I could send you to a nursing home for a week or so, or alternatively you could come back with me."

"To your home?" She sounded very polite but her eyes were suddenly guarded.

"Yes, why not? The moorland air would soon put you right and you'd be a companion for Fay, my daughter."

Her face cleared.

"Oh, you're married. Perhaps your wife would like a governess for the little girl, or—or a companion or something."

"My wife's dead," he said briefly, and she looked embarrassed.

"Oh—oh, I see. Then I could hardly stay in your house with you and just the little girl, could I?"

He smiled reluctantly.

"Well, perhaps it wouldn't do, though Simmy, Fay's governess, would be a most excellent chaperon. However . . . ." He began to pace up and down the room, his hands in his pockets.

Miranda watched him under her lashes, revising her first opinion of him. He looked older in the morning light, considerably older than his thirty-eight years, and he was going a little gray. His patients would like that, she thought, and would also like the suggestion of autocracy in his rather brusque manner. Yes, a great many women would find him attractive.

"You're a bit of a problem, aren't you?" he said, pausing at the foot of the bed where he stood looking down at her. "Can't you get in touch with this Pierre, who seems to be the only friend you have?"

"My letters to Pierre were returned," she said. "His present address is unknown. I think, perhaps, if he is married to Marguerite, she does not wish him to remember his old friends."

"I see. Well, that seems to leave me, and I really cannot have it on my conscience that I turned a child of your tender years and inexperience adrift in the world."

"I do not see why I need be on your conscience," she said. "After all, it was only a chance meeting."

"Still, sometimes chance meetings have their significance," he said slowly, and his hand closed on Grace's letter. "Miranda, did you mean what you said last night about putting security above the independence—above, shall we say, romance?"

"Of course," she said, looking surprised. "But, for someone like me, that can only come through a desirable marriage."

"A desirable marriage," he repeated with a little quirk of the lips. "I wonder if marriage to me would come into that category."

"To you?" For the first time she seemed at a loss for speech while conflicting expressions chased each other across her astonished face.

"You mean . . . you mean . . . but you're not *serious!*"

"Strangely enough, I think I'm perfectly serious," he replied on a faint note of surprise, and removing the breakfast tray from her knees, he came and sat down on the edge of the bed.

CHAPTER TWO

"FIRST OF ALL," he began in his lecture-room manner, "let's get the position quite clear. You need a home and someone to provide for you, I need a mistress for my house and a companion for my child. I also need—especially now—the . . . social protection of a wife."

"Some woman is trying to marry you?" she asked calmly.

He smiled. She had an admirable directness.

"Something like that, though rather more nebulous. Rather, shall we say, a situation has arisen that might become awkward. At the same time I ought to marry again for Fay's sake."

"But I do not think," she said sedately, "that I would make a good mother to a strange little girl."

He regarded her quizzically.

"Perhaps not, but Fay doesn't need a mother. She needs a companion nearer her own age—twelve."

"Seven years difference. Not enough for a stepmother."

"It depends on the point of view," he retorted. "You don't know my daughter yet. Now, there's not much I can tell you about myself. I'm reasonably well-to-do as things go today, and you would find me quite generous."

"But not, perhaps, an easy man to live with," she said gently.

His eyebrows lifted.

"I don't think you'd find me unreasonable. In any case you wouldn't see a great deal of me. I'm an extremely busy man and when there's a rush of work I frequently don't come home at all, and I have an apartment over my consulting rooms for those occasions. Far from finding me under your feet, you might feel a little lonely. The house is very isolated.''

"But one would be unreasonable to expect perfection from such an arrangement," she said.

"A very sensible point of view," he said a little dryly. "Well, what do you say?"

She lay back on the pillows and looked at the ceiling.

"Have you thought, perhaps, that I might not suit you as a wife?" she asked sedately. "Me, I have my own personality. I would not care to be a little dog to do your bidding."

For the first time, he laughed.

"I hope I shouldn't order you to do anything, but if I so far forgot myself then you would have to resemble the little dog still further and snap at my heels."

Her mouth curled up in a grin.

"You're nice when you laugh," she said, and stretched out a hand to him. "I could like you."

He remembered her saying, the night before, that it should not be difficult to make yourself love anyone who was reasonably decent, and moved uneasily.

"I hope you will," he said a little brusquely. "I could like you, too—very much. But don't be under any misapprehension, Miranda. This would be purely a business arrangement."

She withdrew her hand and regarded him gravely.

"Of course. You have made your needs quite clear."

"Well, I'll leave you to think it over. My train leaves at one o'clock, so give me your answer as soon as you're dressed as I'll have to make some sort of arrangement for you."

He got up and she stretched herself slowly.

"There's nothing to think over," she said. "You can have your answer now."

"You mean you've decided against the idea?" For a moment he felt an irrational sense of disappointment.

"Oh, no," she said, and sighed. "I really have no choice, for such an opportunity would never come my way again. Yes, Mr. Chantry, I will marry you. What, please, is your first name?"

"Adam."

"Adam . . ." she repeated slowly. " 'And the Lord God said, It is not good that the man should be alone; I will make him a helpmeet for him. . . .' "

"You're a strange child," he said, smiling. "Now hurry up and get dressed. There are matters to be discussed before I go."

He was writing in the smoking room, a small pile of neatly addressed envelopes on the desk beside him, when she came down. He looked up with a brief smile and waved her to a chair.

"I won't keep you long," he said briskly. "Order some coffee—I've just half an hour before I must leave."

He turned back to his letters. By the time he had finished a waiter had brought the coffee and Miranda was already drinking hers.

"Well, that should take care of everything for the time being," he said, sitting down beside her, the letters in his hand. "Now listen carefully. This is a note to a Miss Evans. She is a retired nurse and runs a very small convalescent home in Hampstead. I've explained the circumstances and she will look after you until I can make other arrangements. Here is a note for my bank. Go and see them. They will have instructions from the Plymouth branch for you to draw on a specified amount. In this envelope you will find my professional address and telephone number and enough money to settle your bill here and cover your fare to London. I have to return here in a week or so to operate, after which I'll meet you in London where we'll get married at once—it'll mean a special license, but the less fuss and publicity we have the better. By the way, I've simply told Miss Evans you are a patient, so I don't advise you to enlighten her in any way. She's a bit of an old gossip. Now, is all this quite clear?"

She sat looking at the letters, her forehead wrinkling a little.

"Yes," she said. "But the bank—I will not need money if I am staying with this Miss Evans."

He regarded her with a certain dry amusement.

"You'll need clothes, my dear child," he said. "If, as you

say, what you have on is all you possess, I hardly think it's an adequate wardrobe to bring with you as a bride.''

"I see," she said, and sat silently turning the letters over in her hands. Then she looked up at him. "You are very trusting, aren't you? I could—make use of these, and then quietly vanish before you returned.''

"That's a chance I have to take," he said with a certain severity, "but I think I'll back my fancy all the same. Now, I must go up and pack and settle my bill. Is there anything else you want to ask me before I go?''

"I don't think so," she said sedately. "Would you like me to come to the station with you?''

"Not in the least," he replied. "I hate being seen off. Have a good lunch here, then go up to London and get settled with Miss Evans.''

She was still sitting in the smoking room, looking a little lost, when he came down ready for his journey.

"Goodbye," he said, holding out his hand. "I'll let you know as soon as all the arrangements have been made. In the meantime, rest as much as you can and make up for all those missed meals, please. I must go now. My taxi's waiting.''

"Goodbye," she said, shaking hands formally. "I hope you have a pleasant journey.''

She did not thank him for his kindness of the night before and he did not seem to expect it. He gave her a brief nod and a smile, and she remained where she was in the smoking room and watched his tall figure cross the lounge and disappear through the swinging doors.

The life of the little hotel went on, ignoring her. It was just on one o'clock. Miranda pinched herself hard and went in to lunch.

TO ADAM the ensuing days were too full for him to give much thought to his approaching marriage. There was pressing work awaiting him on his return, and every hour in his appointment book was filled for the next fortnight so that he was rarely at home and slept, as usual at such times, in the apartment above his consulting rooms. Indeed, when he thought of Miranda at all it was with a mixture of amusement and approval that at nineteen she should take such a practical view of the future. He saw no strangeness in the situation. He was not an impulsive man, but he believed in snap decisions. He had decided on marriage just as he would have decided to operate, and the decision being made, the sooner the thing was accomplished the better for everyone.

The weekend he spent at home only strengthened his purpose. Fay was difficult and demanding, and he saw with sharper clarity that the years of isolation at Wintersbride had made her far too precocious. Grace was not good for her, unconsciously ingratiating herself with the child to establish a footing with the father. Watching Grace among his roses, touching this bloom and that with proprietary fingers, he compared her with Miranda and smiled a little grimly. Miranda was a child. She would never, as the older woman would, remind him of Melisande, gracious, elegant, the perfect chatelaine of his home.

He did not tell them then of his intention to marry, but the evening before he was to return to Maybury-on-sea to operate, he drove out to Wintersbride to pack a few additional things. Fay had gone to bed and, when Miss Simms asked him if he were returning straight home from Maybury, he replied casually, "No, I'm going on to London for a night. I'm getting married."

"Married!" For a moment Simmy looked as taken aback as she felt, and her long sallow face dropped its habitual mask. She admired Grace, but she had not shared the general opinion that Mr. Chantry should marry again.

"It's very sudden, isn't it?" she said, but the colorless lashes hid her eyes.

"Shocks are better sprung suddenly or not at all," he replied enigmatically. "You evidently don't feel it's a matter for congratulations, Simmy."

"I'm sorry, Mr. Chantry," she said quickly. "You took me by surprise. I hope you'll be . . . very happy. Have you told Fay?"

His smile was a little cryptic.

"No. You can do that tomorrow. She'll take it better from you."

Simmy smiled.

"I don't think you need worry. You're here so seldom and Fay is quite fond of Miss Latham."

Adam gave her a level look.

"It's not Miss Latham I'm marrying," he said briefly.

"Not Miss Latham? But I thought . . . ." She looked bewildered.

"Too many people suffer from wishful thinking without any real grounds for it," he said. "None of you knows the lady I'm bringing here, and that, perhaps, is all to the good."

He picked up his suitcase and started to go. He was clearly not going to elaborate further and Miss Simms knew him too well to ask questions.

"Then you won't be returning at once," she said, and he frowned.

"Why not? If you're thinking of honeymoons, Simmy, I'm much too busy for that. We shall be coming straight back. I'll wire you, and in the meantime tell Mrs. Yeo to get the south room ready."

"Very well. Is she to—leave it as it is?"

The south room had been Melisande's. It had not been used since she died, but the books, the expensive trifles and the monogramed toilet set were still there as she had left them.

For a moment his eyes narrowed, and he looked at Miss Simms with passing speculation. What was she going to think of the second Mrs. Chantry?

"Why not?" he said then, and his smile was a little ironical. "Now I come to think of it, the initials are the same. Goodbye, Simmy. I can safely leave everything to you."

As he drove back to Plymouth he remembered Miranda saying, "You're very trusting, aren't you? . . . I could quietly vanish before you return," and it crossed his mind for a moment that he might be making a fool of himself. What did he know of her save that she was a little waif with an unusual philosophy of life? However, there was a letter awaiting him at his apartment, acknowledging his arrangements for their marriage and assuring him that she would be ready for him at the appointed time, and he promptly forgot her as he ran through his secretary's rearrangement of his future appointments.

If Adam had been too preoccupied to give much thought to the situation, for Miranda the days were very different. As she grew stronger under Miss Evans's watchful care, she had plenty of time to reflect. What had seemed practical and possible on an empty stomach appeared, after a course of good food and rest, to be a momentous step to take in such a hurry. What did she know of this stranger, so much older than herself, who could contemplate taking a wife with no more thought than he might give to the choosing of a puppy? She had liked him, and instinctively she had trusted him, but she knew she would have felt the same toward anyone who had come to her rescue at that particular moment.

Lying awake in her narrow, hard little bed, she tried to reason as she had so often heard Pierre reason. Security was important, he had argued. One could become fond of anyone, given the right background and a reasonable nature. She thought that life soon taught one to acquire a reasonable nature and that fondness was a matter of temperament. She could not afford doubts in her present position and, as she herself had said to Adam, such an opportunity might never come her way again, and a marriage of convenience, even with a stranger, could be no worse than the terrifying struggle for existence in a world devoid of friends.

So, from the first doubts Miranda drifted into a dreamlike state of acceptance. She visited Adam's bank, half expecting a polite disclaimer of her existence, but found the friendly manager reassuring and incurious. She delivered Adam's note to an expensive-looking shop in Bruton Street and found herself immediately taken in hand by the head saleswoman.

Here, Adam had presumably made his intentions clear, and the saleswoman was flattering, if a little condescending. It soon became evident that the first Mrs. Chantry had spent lavishly and had been regarded as a privileged customer.

"A very beautiful woman and a real pleasure to dress,"
Miranda was told. "So sad, her sudden death. We were all
desolated here in the salon. We did not think that Mr. Chantry
would ever marry again, but then, time heals old wounds."

Miranda attended numerous fittings, listening politely to the
gossip and wondering if Adam had been deeply in love with his
wife. She was aware that his second choice was occasioning
surprise and veiled curiosity. They were making the best of her,
she thought without resentment. She could not, they told her
kindly, carry off the creations that had made the first Mrs.
Chantry one of the best-dressed women in London, but she
could capitalize on her youth.

Miranda smiled with secret amusement, thinking it was a pity
that so much thought and expense were to be wasted on a man
who would scarcely appreciate it.

Miss Evans became increasingly curious as Miranda's trousseau began to arrive at the nursing home.

"My! Dubonnet's!" she exclaimed, fingering the labels on
the boxes. And her look plainly said that there must be something a little odd about a patient who arrived in a cheap, shabby
suit, with no other luggage, and then proceeded to spend a small
fortune in Bruton Street. "Are you getting married all of a
sudden?"

"Yes," said Miranda, embarrassed. It was better to tell her
that much. "We—my fiancé is buying my trousseau."

"Dear me! Your fiancé must be a rich young man, or are you
just sending him the bills and hoping for the best?"

"He made the arrangement himself," Miranda said a little
stiffly.

"Well, well," Miss Evans said coyly, "some people have all
the luck. Will he be calling for you here when you leave, dear?"

"I don't know," Miranda replied.

She had not yet received Adam's letter telling her to meet him
outside the registrar's office, to please remember the ring as he
did not know the size of her finger.

She visited a jeweler the day before the wedding, feeling
unaccountably depressed. It felt strange and a little lonely to buy

your own wedding ring, and she thought the salesman looked at her oddly as he noticed her hands were bare of any other rings.

"Gold or platinum?" he asked indifferently.

"I don't know. What is usual?" Miranda said.

"It's a matter of taste, madam," the man replied, looking pained. "Platinum is more favored these days. Is your engagement ring set in platinum?"

"My engagement ring? Oh, I haven't got one yet," said Miranda, confused.

The salesman pursed his lips, brought out a tray of plain platinum rings and said firmly, "Madam had better try them for size."

She tried them on hastily until she found one that fitted.

"This will do," she said.

She paid for the ring quickly and was glad to get out of the shop. She was sure that the man was quite convinced by now that her intentions were not strictly matrimonial.

She turned with relief into a neighboring café, and as she sat at the marble-topped table, she realized fully for the first time that tomorrow by this time she would be married to a stranger and journeying toward a home of which she did not even know the name.

SHE GOT UP EARLY the next morning to do her packing. She had bought as little as possible, but even so she seemed to possess more clothes than she had ever owned before.

What did one wear at a wedding in a registrar's office on a cold summer's day, she wondered, surveying her new finery doubtfully. In the end she chose a plain linen dress with a childish round collar because the color reminded her of the Mediterranean. She had no idea that it turned her at once into a well-dressed schoolgirl.

She had spent so long deciding what to wear that she was late for her appointment. Adam, waiting outside the registrar's office, frowned at his watch and wondered again if she had made a fool of him, then he saw her running down the street. He had time to watch her before she saw him and his eyes narrowed in cynical impatience with himself. Why, she was just a child! He should be taking out adoption papers, not signing the marriage register.

"You're late," he said in the same peremptory tones he used to his nurses when he had been kept waiting.

She stood before him, breathless and a little flushed. She looked up at the dark, unfamiliar face, at the strong lines of self-discipline, at the gray in his hair, and for a moment her resolution faltered.

"I'm sorry," she said. "I could not find a taxi."

"Well, come along. We're twenty minutes late already. Have you got the ring?"

Dumbly she fumbled for it in her purse, and he saw her hand tremble as she gave it to him. For a moment he must have understood her panic, for he said, looking down at her with a softening of the dark, probing gaze, "Are you sure you want to go through with this? It's not too late to change your mind."

She took a deep breath.

"Yes, I'm sure—as sure as I've been of anything since my father died."

She felt his hand on her shoulder for an instant.

"It will be all right," he said. "This next quarter of an hour doesn't mean anything. Just think of it as signing a contract—a contract for a better job than you've had so far. That's all it means to me, you know."

"Yes, of course."

It did not seem like a marriage ceremony. The registrar with his professional smile, the two strange witnesses, even the words she spoke, were quite unreal. Very quickly the ring was on her finger and the registrar was raising his eyebrows because the bridegroom showed no signs of kissing the bride. Then they were out in the street again and Adam was on the curb, flagging a taxi.

"Did you notice his false teeth?" Miranda said as the taxi took them to the nursing home to collect her luggage. "I thought they would come unstuck any minute."

"Never got beyond his temporary set, I expect," Adam

replied. It was the only conversation they had before they reached Hampstead.

Miss Evans greeted Adam effusively, and her eyes bulged when she realized that it was he whom her uncommunicative little patient had been engaged to marry. She followed Miranda up to her room and stood a little grimly in the doorway while the cases were shut and locked.

"Well!" she remarked. "You *are* a deep one and no mistake. Why couldn't you have told me it was Adam Chantry you were going to marry? Cradle snatching, that's what I call it, but they're all the same after they've reached a certain age. Not that I'm not pleased he's married again. He's still a comparatively young man, and although he was so passionately in love with his first wife, I always say, time heals old wounds."

"Mrs. Chantry was a very beautiful woman, so I understand," Miranda said, locking the last of the suitcases.

"Quite the beauty," replied Mrs. Evan promptly. "I only saw her once, but she was like something out of the pictures— and how he worshipped her! I shouldn't have said you'd be his cup of tea, but you never can tell, can you?"

"I must go," Miranda said, her color high at the woman's expression. "We have a train to catch."

They had lunch on the train. The waiter was deferential but alluded to Miranda as the young lady, and Adam remarked with a sardonic grin, "You'll have to get used to being taken for my niece, or even my daughter."

She smiled at him a little uneasily. She had not as yet thought of herself as his wife.

The journey seemed endless. Adam was considerate, but he was not disposed to talk, and she sat opposite him for hours, looking out the window.

It was a long time later when, having dropped to sleep, she opened her eyes at a sudden lurch the train gave, and found he was watching her speculatively.

"You look better," he said approvingly.

"Better?"

"Than when we first met, though there's still plenty of

improvement we can effect. You're too thin and I should say
you still need plenty of rest."

"I've always been thin," she said. "Does—does your little
girl mind about me?"

His smile was a little crooked.

"I haven't the slightest idea. I left her governess to tell her."

"Oh . . . ." She looked at him under her lashes. Did he
think, she wondered, the child would resent her? "How old was
she when her mother died?"

"Five."

"Then she remembers her?"

"Hardly. Her mother was ill for some time. The child was
sent away." His lips still had that bitter little quirk, but his eyes
were hard and guarded. He clearly did not want to be ques-
tioned, and presently he picked up a book and began to read.

Seven years, Miranda thought, watching his square,
surgeon's hands as they turned the pages; seven years in which
to grieve for a beautiful woman. But the lines in his face spelled
bitterness and self-discipline rather than grief, and he had not,
she thought, learned tolerance from the past.

She was tired by the time they reached Plymouth, and was
glad she had not packed her coat as she followed Adam into the
station yard and stood shivering beside the luggage while he
went to look for his chauffeur.

She thought the man looked at her with surprise as he touched
his cap, but she was becoming used to that, and to Adam's long
silences. He sat beside her in the car without speaking as they
were driven out of the town and through the dim, misty drizzle
to the edge of Dartmoor. Every so often the mist lifted sufficiently for her to catch a glimpse of the rough, desolate country
that seemed to stretch in unbroken solitude as far as the darken-
ing horizon.

Once, as she shivered, he asked her if she was cold, and when
she shook her head he remarked casually, "You'll get used to
Dartmoor. You're not seeing it at its best this evening."

"Does anyone live here?" she asked, and he smiled at the
doubt in her voice.

"Oh, yes. There are farms and little villages, and there's Wintersbride."

"Wintersbride?" She lingered over the curious name.

"Your home."

"Oh," she said, and withdrew farther into her corner.

It was too misty to see much by the time they arrived at the house, but she had an impression of well-kept lawns and terraces. The house itself was big and sprawling and built of the harsh west-country stone, a silent forbidding house with shuttered windows that revealed no lights.

"Welcome to Wintersbride," Adam said a little sardonically as the car stopped, and she shivered. His touch was light and impersonal as he helped her out of the car. He looked at her for a moment with a quizzical expression. "You don't like it?" he asked politely.

"It has a—a secret look" she said, staring at the blind windows.

"I hope you're not fanciful, Miranda," he replied a little shortly, and even as he spoke the front door was opened from within and light flooded out, dispelling the illusion.

She followed Adam up the short flight of steps and stood blinking in the light while she listened to him greeting the tall, thin woman who had opened the door.

"Well, here we are, Simmy, right on schedule. All well?"

"Yes, Mr. Chantry. Fay will be down in a moment. It's very late, I know, but we made an exception this evening."

"Miranda, this is Miss Simms, Fay's governess, and the mainstay of this house. Simmy, this is my wife."

For the first time, Miss Simms looked at Miranda thoroughly, observing the immature figure, the young, transparent face, and the pale soft hair that curled so childishly. Miss Simms's eyes, which at first had held a shock of dismay, changed to a look of condescension before they were veiled again with her habitual reserve.

"How do you do?" said Miranda, holding out her hand.

"Forgive me," the governess replied, shaking hands after a barely perceptible pause. "You are so much younger than we had expected, Mrs. Chantry. I'm happy to welcome you to Wintersbride.''

Her touch was cold, and Miranda thought there was hostility in the quiet voice, or was it only polite surprise? She was aware of Adam's frown as he watched them both. He turned to the foot of the staircase and called in peremptory tones, "Fay! Come down at once!''

There was a movement on the landing above and Miranda realized that someone had been there listening all the time. Slowly a figure began to descend the stairs, and as the light fell on a child's face, so strange, so darkly beautiful, she caught her breath.

"Come along and get acquainted," Adam said. "You should have been down here with Simmy to welcome your stepmother, you know."

The child continued her slow descent. On the bottom step she paused and her dark, brilliant gaze fastened on Miranda, who was standing alone, a little forlornly, in the center of the hall.

"*You*—my stepmother!" she said, and began to laugh.

"Fay, remember your manners, please," Miss Simms said sharply, but the child turned and fled back up the stairs and the peals of her derisive laughter came echoing down to them until a door slammed somewhere and there was silence.

CHAPTER THREE

MIRANDA, GETTING READY for bed in the strange bedroom that seemed so uncomfortably large, gazed into her own eyes, which, wide and apprehensive, looked back at her from the mirror.

Her nerve had been shaken by that wild laughter, and there had been something hostile about all three of them at that moment—the child running away, the governess displeased but unsurprised, and Adam, his dark face cold and taut as his brooding gaze rested critically on Miranda's motionless figure.

"Fay is a precocious child," he had said then. "She probably thinks you're not much older than she is. Simmy will show you your room. You'd like a bath before dinner, I daresay."

She had wondered if Miss Simms thought it strange that Adam should not himself perform that small courtesy for his bride, but following the governess up the wide, polished staircase, she received the unwelcome impression that Simmy knew all that went on in the house.

A maid was already in the bedroom unpacking, and Miss Simms said, "This is Nancy. She looks after Fay's needs and yours, too, of course, from now on. You have only to ring. Nancy, I'm sure you'll make Mrs. Chantry comfortable."

The girl stared with ill-concealed curiosity. She had bold eyes, but she looked friendly and Miranda smiled at her and received a knowing grin in return before she was left alone with the governess. Miranda wandered over to the dressing table and her eyes fell on the monogramed brushes gleaming with polished elegance in the lamplight.

"Oh," she cried, "how lovely," and felt surprise that Adam should have taken thought or time to prepare for her coming.

In the mirror she saw the governess's mouth tighten, and on an impulse she turned and said shyly, "I do hope you will like me, Miss Simms—you and the little girl."

Miss Simms did not answer directly, but replied with a faint air of reproof, "You must excuse Fay tonight, Mrs. Chantry. She was not prepared. It would have been better if her father had explained the circumstances to her himself."

"The circumstances?"

"The fact that you were so young. I'm afraid the child has been building up the wrong sort of picture of you."

"Oh, I see. Well, I do not think I was prepared, either. She's lovely, isn't she?"

"She's very like her mother," Miss Simms replied colorlessly. "Now, you have your own bathroom—this door here; the other leads to Mr. Chantry's room. Dinner is usually at eight o'clock, but tonight it is put back until nine."

Miranda stood in the middle of the room when the governess had gone and looked at the door that led to the other room. There was a key in the lock, but the door was not locked. So this had been the first Mrs. Chantry's room, she thought. Did he not mind turning it over to a stranger? There must be so many other rooms in the house that one would have thought . . . . She went into the bathroom and turned on the taps with impatience at her own reflections. She or another? What could it matter to Adam Chantry in such circumstances?

No one came to fetch her, and when she heard the gong ring she started down the silent staircase, wondering which room she should try to find first. But Adam was waiting for her at the foot of the stairs and she thought he watched her descent with a quizzical expression.

"We can spare five minutes for a cocktail," he said, and took her into a small paneled room that he said he preferred to use when he was alone.

He gave her a dry martini, then stood appraising her over the rim of his own glass.

"Yes," he said with a little twist to his lips. "I can quite understand how you must strike Simmy."

She looked at him inquiringly, then her wide mouth turned up in an uncertain smile. She had put on a gray chiffon dress with a cherry sash, and at the last moment she had tied a narrow cherry ribbon around her head because it gave her confidence.

"Clothes do make a difference, don't they?" she said a little nervously.

"Dubonnet's have excellent taste," he replied. "Unfortunately you look more like my daughter than my wife."

She could not decide whether he was annoyed or merely amused, so she ventured a little timidly, "Well, it does not much matter either way, does it?"

He put down his empty glass.

"Not a bit," he said briskly. "Shall we go in to dinner?"

It was with relief that she learned that the governess never joined him for dinner, but as each course was placed before her and she sought a little desperately for topics of conversation, she began to feel that the presence of a third person might have made the situation easier. He answered courteously enough such questions as she asked him, but he seemed indisposed to make small talk and at last she fell silent, watching his dark, withdrawn face.

Coffee was brought to the small room where they had drunk their cocktails. She poured it out, conscious that his thoughts were already preoccupied with his work and with the telephone that rang constantly in his study, and she was scarcely surprised when a little later he told her he had an hour or so of writing to put in before he went to bed and would say good-night.

"You'll find plenty of books in that room across the hall," he told her, getting to his feet, "but I would advise going to bed early. It's been a long day and you aren't entirely fit yet."

"Yes," she said. "What time do you have breakfast?"

"I'll be gone before there's any need for you to wake. I'll tell them to send up a tray."

"I see." Her eyes were on her wedding ring, which she was turning round and round on her thin finger. "Are you going away?"

He raised his eyebrows.

"Only into Plymouth. I'll be back in the evening."

"I did not know," she said.

He looked at her bent head, at the absurd ribbon circling her curls like a child's, and he rubbed his chin with a rueful gesture.

"I haven't been very clever about this, have I, Miranda?" he said. "You know nothing about me—my way of life, my tastes, even my working hours."

"Your tastes are probably particular," she said sedately. "But you must remember this is only the second time we have met."

He regarded her silently for a moment, thinking what a strange girl she was, one minute a child, and the next so oddly self-possessed.

"I hope," he said, "that I haven't forced you into taking a step that should have required more thought."

She looked up at him then and her eyes were clear and grave.

"I did not have to marry you," she said. "I would have found some way to live."

He frowned. "You're very young," he said uneasily. "Perhaps I had no right to tie you up in a loveless marriage."

She lowered her lashes.

"It's too late to think of that now," she said. "And you did not strike me at all as the kind of man to indulge in doubts."

"You're very sensible—and astonishingly unromantic for nineteen," he said a little dryly.

"I told you I was not romantic," she said then. "I was not brought up to be."

"That's just as well," he replied. "There's a great deal to be said for the French approach to these things. Well, I really must say good-night. Tomorrow, Simmy or Fay will show you around. Ask Simmy anything you need to know. She's been with us ten years and knows all the ropes. We don't see many people out here, but a Miss Latham may call on you in a day or two. She can tell you all about the neighborhood."

"Is she the entanglement?" asked Miranda simply.

"Entanglement?"

"You said you needed a wife—as a social protection."

"There's no entanglement," he said, frowning. "Grace Latham was a friend of my first wife and is our nearest neighbor, that's all."

"I see."

Aware that he had spoken sharply, he touched her lightly on the shoulder.

"Well, get a good night's rest and ring for anything you happen to want. Good night."

"Good night," she answered, and after he had gone she put out the lights and went upstairs to bed.

And now she sat looking into her mirror and listening to the owls while she reminded herself that this was her wedding night and the house did not welcome her. Wintersbride . . . a strange name, a cold, forbidding name, or was it simply a sad name promising no gladness from such a union as she had made? But long ago in this house, in this same room, the first Mrs. Chantry had awaited her husband's coming and known herself loved.

SHE SLEPT LATE the next morning and awoke to the steady sound of rain. Nancy had placed a breakfast tray beside the bed and was pulling back the heavy curtains.

"Good morning, Nancy. Another wet day?" Miranda said.

"Proper old misery," the girl replied cheerfully. She came now and stood at the foot of the bed, regarding Miranda with frank curiosity. The master's sudden remarriage had created much interest and speculation in the servants' hall, though Mrs. Yeo, the cook-housekeeper who had been in service at Wintersbride in the first Mrs. Chantry's time, had turned down her mouth and said no good would come of it. They had all thought Miss Latham would have been the master's choice and it was plain that no one, not even Miss Simms, had ever heard of this little bit of a thing not much older, by the looks of her, than Miss Fay herself.

"I hope you slept well, ma'am," the girl said demurely, but her eyes strayed to the uncreased pillow beside Miranda's.

Miranda felt herself flushing.

"Very well, thank you," she said briskly. "Will you please give me my bed jacket before you go?"

Left alone, she sat frowning at her breakfast and wondering how many servants Adam kept. Miss Simms must take her to the kitchen and introduce her to the staff. There must be plenty of activity in a house of this size, she thought, and the first thing she could do for Adam would be to see that it was well run.

When she had finished her breakfast she went to the window and looked out. She had got little impression of the countryside the evening before save one of rather bleak desolation, and now as she looked she shivered, for the bleakness and the desolation remained. Beyond the rough wall that bounded the grounds the moor stretched in unbroken solitude as far as the eye could see. Sky and moor were a uniform gray, chill, forbidding and utterly alien to her eyes, and this great gray house was part of the desolation.

She dressed slowly, wondering where she would find Miss Simms at this hour of the morning. It did not occur to her to ring for a servant and ask. Her room was one of several in a short corridor. At the end of the corridor, two steps took her down into another wide passage with doors, and here at last she caught the muffled sound of voices. For a moment she hesitated, wondering if this might be the servants' quarters, but a child's laugh reassured her, and she knocked on one of the doors and heard Simmy's precise voice bid her enter.

She found herself in what was evidently Fay's schoolroom and wondered for a moment why, with so many rooms to choose from, Adam had picked this small, square, ugly room on the north side of the house. The window had nursery bars that gave it a cell-like appearance and the furniture was the modern tubular variety found in offices and cocktail bars.

"Good morning, Mrs. Chantry. Did you want anything?" Miss Simms asked, rising politely.

"I was looking for you," Miranda said with a smile. "I thought perhaps you—or Fay—would take me around the house, show me the ropes, in fact."

"After lunch, while Fay is having her rest, I'll be at your disposal," the governess said.

"But can we not go now—all three of us?" asked Miranda impulsively. "It is such a sad morning and I am sure Fay would like some coffee or something when we have done our rounds."

"Simmy will call that sucking up," said Fay in her clear, high voice.

"Don't be rude, dear," Miss Simms said automatically, but her long, sallow face was not a bit disconcerted as she turned to regard Miranda with a calm eye. "I cannot interrupt the lesson, I'm afraid, Mrs. Chantry. We consider routine to be very important at Wintersbride. You will find there is a fire in the small study. Luncheon is at one o'clock."

Miranda felt like a rebuked child and was fully aware of Fay's enjoyment of her discomfiture.

"I'm sorry," she said. "How do I find the kitchen quarters, please?"

"The kitchen?" Simmy's eyebrows rose. "I don't think this would be a very good moment—"

"Surely it is quite usual to visit one's kitchen in the mornings," Miranda said gently. "To give the orders for the day, I mean."

"The orders for the day? Oh, you are referring to meals. You've no need to trouble about anything like that, Mrs. Chantry. Mrs. Yeo—she's been cook-housekeeper here for years—does all that. Mrs. Chantry—I beg your pardon, I should have said the *late* Mrs. Chantry—left everything to Mrs. Yeo."

"I see," said Miranda, feeling chilled.

"If you would care to see Mrs. Yeo, I will send her to you in the small study," Miss Simms said, but Miranda turned to the door.

"No, it does not matter," she replied, and went away.

The late Mrs. Chantry . . . it was the first time Miranda was to hear that phrase from a member of the household, and even then the shadow of Melisande touched her with momentary disquiet.

She began to explore the ground-floor rooms for herself. There were not so many as she had at first supposed, and they all bore a curious uniform resemblance. The dark dining room, the small, well-stocked library, even the little paneled study, which last night had seemed friendlier with its wood fire and faded tapestry upholstery, had a secret air of anonymity, as if the facades they presented did not reveal their true personalities. Miranda made a face, remembering Adam's expressed hope that she was not fanciful, and she looked into the room in which the telephone had kept ringing, which she knew must be his study. She opened the door, half expecting to find a replica of the chromium fittings upstairs, but the room was like all the rest, admirably equipped with good period pieces; the desk and the modern filing cabinet had been chosen with care, and the neatness of the room bore mute witness to Adam's well-ordered habits.

There was one room left, and as Miranda opened the door and stood for a moment on the threshold, she immediately received a different impression. This was clearly the drawing room, though the holland covers that draped the furniture proclaimed that it was not in use. Even so, the room had a quality the others lacked, and as Miranda whipped off dust sheets to see what lay beneath, it began to reveal itself in all its graciousness. The rest of the house held good taste and quiet comfort, but whoever had designed this room was an artist, and Miranda's gaze was drawn to the portrait that hung above the fireplace at the farther end.

She walked slowly across the room and the lovely face of the first Mrs. Chantry came sharply into focus like a camera shot on the screen. It could be no one else. There were Fay's dark eyes, brilliant and demanding, the full, passionate mouth and the hint of arrogance in the lifted chin and the faint smile that touched the lips. It was the face of a woman secure in the knowledge of her own power, and her beauty was almost insolent in its perfection. This, then, was Adam's wife.

For a moment, as she gazed up at the picture, Miranda experienced a sharp pang of inadequacy, a curious sense of trespass in her hsuband's house, and she jumped guiltily as a voice said sharply from the doorway, "What are you doing in there?"

MIRANDA WALKED SLOWLY to the door, her eyes resting curiously on the tall, motionless young woman who stood there with her arms full of flowers.

"Who are you?" she asked.

"I'm Miss Latham," the older woman replied. "Who are you?"

Miranda grinned.

"I'm the new Mrs. Chantry," she said.

Miss Latham was too polite to gaze incredulously, but she could not altogether keep the dismay out of her fine eyes.

"I beg your pardon," she said quickly, "I took you for a maid at first. I walked in, I'm afraid. Adam and I are old friends."

Miranda glanced at her sharply. Yes, this must be the entanglement. She had a proprietary air, and the way she had said "Adam and I are old friends" was slightly self-conscious.

"How do you do, Miss Latham. Adam told me you would be calling," she said demurely.

"Oh, please—I hope you'll call me Grace," the other woman said with a little laugh. "And you—what's your name?"

"Miranda."

"Miranda . . . . Well, Miranda, I came over at once to welcome the bride. The news was so very sudden that I wasn't able to get over and arrange some flowers for you, but I've brought you these."

"Thank you."

Miranda took the flowers and stood holding them awkwardly. If Grace Latham was disconcerted by Adam's unexpected marriage to a stranger she hid it very well and, as she observed Miranda more closely, her natural poise grew more assured.

"Why, you're only a child!" she exclaimed in her soft, deep voice. "Whatever was Adam thinking of?"

. "I'm nineteen," said Miranda, amused. "And he is not
really so old, you know."

"Of course not, but nearly twenty years' difference . . . oh,
well, I'm sure you'll be a great surprise to all his friends,"
Grace said, and her gaze shifted involuntarily to the portrait over
the fireplace.

"Do you think so?" Miranda began to feel irritated. "Shall
we go into the other room? There is a fire there."

"Hadn't we better replace the dust covers first?" Grace asked
gently, but Miranda did not give the room another glance.

"Leave them," she said. "The room will have to be thoroughly cleaned and aired before it is used, anyway."

Grace followed her into the small study and said, a little
diffidently, "Are you thinking of using the drawing room again,
then?"

Miranda put down the flowers in a careless heap on a table.
"But of course. It is the nicest room in the house."

"She planned it," Grace said with a sigh. "Adam's first
wife, you know. She had exquisite taste. The room has never
been used since she died."

"Not for seven years? How absurd! But then I do not suppose
a man alone would have much use for a drawing room," said
Miranda cheerfully.

But Grace replied with gentle reproach, "Forgive me, but
you probably don't understand. Adam felt his wife's death very
deeply. Anything that helped to remind him—well, it's natural,
isn't it?"

"The whole house would remind him if it comes to that,"
retorted Miranda, thinking of the south room that was now hers.
"Why did he not sell the place at the time?"

"There was Fay, you see."

"A child can adjust to being transplanted. She was only
five."

"It wasn't as easy as that. Fay has never been very strong,
and Adam thought it best for her to grow up here. Hasn't he
talked to you about these things?"

"We have not had time to discuss anything much," Miranda replied before she could stop herself. "We have only met twice."

Grace's well-modeled eyebrows rose.

"My dear child! What on earth do you mean?"

"Exactly what I say. I met him once a fortnight ago, and yesterday when I married him."

At last Grace Latham's poise was punctured. The fool, the utter fool, she thought angrily . . . Adam Chantry of all men to be caught by a scheming little adventuress. . . .

"Where did you meet him?" she asked coldly, and did not realize how plainly her feelings showed on her face.

But Miranda had had enough of her visitor. If Adam had married her as an escape from this she was not going to put up with being patronized.

"I met him at a fair," she said jauntily.

"A fair—*Adam*?" Grace was nearly routed then. "Do you mean you—picked him up?"

Miranda considered.

"Well, I suppose you could call it that. Actually, he picked me up—quite literally off the ground in the tent of the Mighty Mesmero—but I do not suppose you have ever heard of him."

Grace got to her feet.

"It all sounds utter nonsense, and highly unlike Adam," she said, then eyed Miranda more closely. "Or were you, perhaps, pulling my leg?"

"Oh, no, I was not," said Miranda innocently. "Will you stay to lunch, Miss Latham?"

"No—no, thank you," said Grace hastily. "I'm expected home for luncheon. Will you tell Adam I called? I—my mother is giving a little dinner party for you one evening soon."

"That will be very nice—I'll tell my husband," said Miranda politely, and accompanied her guest to the door.

As she watched Grace's car move off in the rain she experienced an unwonted sense of depression. She should not have sent her away with such a startling impression, and she suspected that Adam would not be pleased if he knew. Well, it was too late now. She had been childish and indiscreet, but there had been something about Grace Latham all along that had rubbed her the wrong way. The gong sounded somewhere in the house, and she turned reluctantly to face the fresh ordeal of lunch with Miss Simms and the child.

It was an uncomfortable meal. The governess insisted that Miranda sit in Adam's place at the head of the table, but she regarded her with the same watchful eye that she kept on her charge. Fay was sullen and picked at her food and Miss Simms made academic small talk that proved rather exhausting.

Only once did the child volunteer a statement, and that was when Miranda mentioned that Grace Latham had called.

"Why didn't you ask her for lunch?" she demanded.

"I did ask her, but she had to get back," Miranda replied.

"But didn't she want to see *me*?"

"She did not suggest it."

"Of course she wanted to! Don't think," said Fay, brandishing her knife and fork, "that because *you've* come here you can keep Grace out. My father won't stand for that."

"You are very fond of Miss Latham, perhaps?" suggested Miranda.

"I love her, I love her, I love her!" the little girl screamed, stamping her feet. Then she burst into tears.

"Fay, go up to the schoolroom like a good child. I'll come to you later," Miss Simms said, and to Miranda's surprise, the child obeyed her at once.

"Goodness!" exclaimed Miranda. "Does she often do that?"

Miss Simms went on eating as if nothing had happened. "She's highly strung," she replied unemotionally. "We sometimes have these little storms. It's best to take no notice."

"Is she really so devoted to Miss Latham?" Miranda asked curiously.

The governess lowered her eyes.

"She's fond of her, yes. But Fay's affections tend to change with her circumstances," she said.

It was an ambiguous remark and Miranda was not sure if it was intended as a warning or not.

"Perhaps," she said, feeling her way, "she needs other children to play with."

Miss Simms looked at her then.

"There are very few children of the right age around here," she said tonelessly, "and Fay is not a good mixer."

"Well," said Miranda reasonably, "how can she learn to be a good mixer if she never meets anyone?"

"You had better talk to Mr. Chantry about these matters," Miss Simms said, her pale eyes veiled once again in reserve, and Miranda felt herself politely dismissed.

They finished their lunch in silence, and Miss Simms declined coffee.

"If you will excuse me, I will go and settle Fay for her hour's rest," she said. "After that I am at your disposal, should you want me for anything."

"I do not think so, unless—would it be possible for one of the maids to air out the drawing room?" Miranda asked.

Simmy stiffened.

"The drawing room?" she repeated with raised eyebrows. "That's a room we never use."

"Well, it's different now, isn't it?" Miranda said pleasantly. "I shall use it myself if no one else wants to."

"Mrs. Chantry—" the governess spoke repressively "—the servants have instructions not to meddle with that room."

"Whose instructions?" asked Miranda coolly.

"The late Mrs. Chantry's," Miss Simms replied, equally coolly. "No one entered that room then except by her express invitation."

"But," Miranda protested incredulously, "she is dead! She has been dead seven years!"

"Yes, she's dead," said Simmy, colorlessly. "Now perhaps you will excuse me."

Left alone, Miranda experienced a swift wave of rebellion. Did Simmy think she could treat her by the same controlled methods she used with the child? And what was all this nonsense about the wishes of a woman who had been dead for seven years? She had a sudden impression of Grace Latham's deep voice saying with gentle reproof, "Adam felt his wife's death very deeply. Anything that helped to remind him . . . ." And the mood passed. She was, she told herself, only a guest in her husband's house, and she could not complain of matters that she did not understand.

She went back to the drawing room, meaning to have another look inside, but the door was locked and someone had removed the key.

CHAPTER FOUR

BY THE TIME Adam returned in the evening, Miranda had tabulated in her mind the things she wished to speak to him about, but somehow they did not get said. Adam seemed preoccupied and brusque and his manner did not encourage suggestions that might sound a little like interference on such short acquaintance.

Such short acquaintance . . . . Miranda observed him covertly. He seemed very professional in his dark clothes, with the gray in his hair and the deeply marked lines that gave his face the look of a much older man; professional and not nearly so approachable as he had appeared that night of the fair. She moved uneasily and he looked at her suddenly over his paper with that penetrating, considering glance that she was coming to know.

"You have the unusual gift of knowing when to refrain from chattering, haven't you?" he said.

"Gentlemen do not like to be disturbed when reading the newspaper," she told him gravely.

He smiled and put the paper down.

"Very true," he said. "But I should have taken more interest in your first day at Wintersbride."

"It rained all day," she said, rejecting the moment as unpropitious for the things she had meant to say. "I learned the geography of the house and Miss Latham came to call."

He frowned.

"Oh, yes. What on earth possessed you to give her that garbled account of that night at the fair?"

"How did you know?" she asked, with curiosity rather than dismay.

"She phoned me at my office."

"Oh. . . ."

"To warn me to give you a hint not to spread the story among my colleagues and patients."

"I do not know your colleagues and patients," she replied sedately. "Anyway, it was true, wasn't it?"

He did not smile.

"Not the impression you gave Grace. I hope you're not an *enfant terrible*, Miranda. Naiveness is so tiresome."

"I'm sorry," she said meekly. "Perhaps I did want to shock her. She treated me like a little girl."

"She was probably only being kind," he told her shortly. "Please remember that she's an old friend and can be very helpful to you in adapting yourself to your new life."

She looked at him under her lashes. Men were very obtuse, she reflected without surprise. It was Grace, she was sure, from whom he had been running away. Did he imagine that because he had now safeguarded himself her feelings would immediately alter?

"I'll remember," she said.

He finished in his lecture-room voice, "I entertain and am entertained very little, but there are certain people you will be expected to meet. I hope you will remember not to indulge in fairy tales. There has been enough talk as it is."

"You have had a—difficult day?" she suggested tentatively, and he smiled with more naturalness.

"Human curiosity is proverbial and I suppose I asked for it by keeping my marriage so much in the dark. I'll have to put you on view sometime, you know."

"Isn't that what you married me for?" she said politely. "A social protection—the conventional wife to be sometimes on view?"

"The arrangement was to our mutual advantage, I thought," he said dryly. "You, I understood, were badly in need of a home."

"I do not reproach you, Adam," she replied gravely, "but

perhaps you are thinking that you did not choose so wisely for your part of the bargain.''

He leaned across and patted her on the knee.

"Silly child," he said, unexpectedly dropping his stiff manner. "I've no doubt it will all work out admirably. Now, tell me, have you made friends with Fay?"

"There has not been much opportunity," she replied evasively. "All the morning she did lessons in that horrible schoolroom, and after lunch she rests and I do not see her again."

"Didn't you have tea together?"

"No. Miss Simms did not permit it. There was, you see, a little trouble at lunch."

His dark eyes rested on her with a guarded expression.

"Oh? What sort of trouble?"

"She was disappointed that Miss Latham did not stay for lunch."

"Oh, is that all? I'm afraid Fay is rather given to tantrums when she doesn't get what she wants. I was hoping you'd be good for her."

"I don't think she likes me. She seems very devoted to Miss Latham."

"She'll expect you to call her Grace, you know," he said with an unexpected twinkle, and added, "Fay's affections are inclined to be subject to her needs. There was a time when she resented Grace very much."

"When she thought she might have her for a stepmother?" asked Miranda calmly, but he only smiled.

"Children get odd notions," he replied. "Why did you describe the schoolroom as horrible?"

"Well, all that chromium furniture and the bars on the window, and it's small and gets no sun. . . ." Her thin hands began to gesticulate. "There are so many unused rooms in the house, Adam, why—"

His eyes were cold and guarded again.

"We consider this is the best room for Fay," he said briefly, and added, "I hope you won't interfere with Simmy's routine, Miranda."

Miranda was silent, and he said with a reluctant smile, "Simmy has a governessy manner. I'm afraid you rather knocked her endways when I brought you home last night. She wasn't expecting anything quite so juvenile."

He thinks I am a child still, she thought, with surprise at such a misconception in a man accustomed to dealing with the ills and demands of humanity.

But after dinner Adam appeared to think he had been a little casual in his dealings with his new bride, for he sent for the servants and introduced them meticulously to Miranda: Nancy, whom she had already met, and Bessie, the parlor maid, and Mrs. Yeo. He apologized majestically for the absence of the gardener and of the girl from the village who helped in the scullery. The latter was very concerned at the moment that she had been caught unprepared and had not had time to change into her housekeeper's black.

"I would have been up before, madam," she said, "but I hope I know my place, and no one asked for me."

Oh, dear, thought Miranda nervously, *she is offended. Adam should have done this last night.*

"I would have come to see you this morning, Mrs. Yeo," she said, "but Miss Simms thought you would be busy."

"Miss Simms should have sent for me," the woman replied. "She knows very well I'd not expect to see you in the kitchen. However, I'm sure I wish you to be very happy, and you, too, sir."

"Thank you," Miranda said, then added more firmly, "Will you come and see me tomorrow morning after breakfast, please, Mrs. Yeo? Just to discuss the meals and any other little thing, you know."

"The *meals*, madam?" Mrs. Yeo's flat face was outraged. "When my lady was alive—begging your pardon, sir—the meals and everything else was left to me. Never a complaint did she make, and the house has been run the same way ever since, isn't that right, sir?"

"If Mrs. Chantry wishes to order the meals herself, you will, I hope, give her every assistance, Mrs. Yeo," Adam said pleasantly. "That will be all for now, thank you. Good night."

"Very good, sir. Good night, sir—madam." Mrs. Yeo's voice was expressionless and she did not look at Miranda again.

"Thank you, Adam, for coming to my rescue," Miranda laughed when the door had closed on them all. "She is very touchy, isn't she?"

"I could do no less than support you," he replied a little curtly. "But I don't advise poaching on Mrs. Yeo's preserves. She's very jealous of her rights."

"But I thought—do you not want me to take any interest in the running of your house?"

"If it will amuse you to play at keeping house, then don't let me or Mrs. Yeo discourage you," he told her gently. "I only meant that I don't expect you to bother your head about such dull things as housekeeping when there is no need."

"Then what do you expect of me?" she asked, trying to find some way in which she might be useful and yet still please him.

"I expect very little," he answered gravely. "Just the common tolerance required when two people have to share the same roof—friendship if you wish it. Is that enough for you Miranda, or are you finding I drove too hard a bargain?"

"No," she said a shade forlornly. "It is you who get so little from your bargain."

"I'm getting all I asked for so far, even though I'm beginning to feel I've asked for too much."

"Or too little."

He moved uneasily.

"Well, let's agree, shall we, that neither of us demand too much of the other?" he said with a little warning inflection in his voice. "Your job for the moment is to make friends with Fay, and that will keep you occupied."

He tried to speak lightly, but he was aware all the time that she was giving him the polite attention of a child who is being talked down to.

He suddenly held out both hands to her.

"Forgive me, Miranda, for my clumsy approaches," he said

with unexpected charm. "I haven't got the hang of you yet. We must get to know each other, mustn't we?"

Her face was tender with swift response as she put her hands in his.

"Ah, yes, Adam," she said. "And I do not think you clumsy. It is just that you cannot decide if I am a child or a woman."

He looked down at the fair head that barely reached his shoulder, and his eyes twinkled.

"I didn't marry you because I thought you were a woman," he told her with gentle mockery.

She turned abruptly from him, withdrawing her hands from his friendly grasp, and would not let him see that he had hurt her.

As she got ready for bed that night she could hear him moving about in his room next door, and already she envied him the work that took him away from Wintersbride all day, and often, as he had told her, all night. And she began to wonder what she was to find to do with the empty hours in this big silent house while the rain drove perpetually across the moor.

THE RAIN had stopped by the morning, but toward evening the mist that had been gathering all day became a thick moor fog and Adam telephoned to say he would stay the night in Plymouth. Miranda dined alone in the chilly dining room, too shy to ask Simmy to keep her company, and when she had finished she went upstairs to see if Fay was asleep yet. A light showed under the door and Miranda knocked and went in.

Fay was in bed reading a paperback novel propped against her knees, and as Miranda came into the room she thrust the book under her pillow.

"Hello," Miranda said, "I thought I'd see if you were asleep yet."

"Did Simmy send you spying?" asked Fay.

"No, why should she? I'm alone tonight, and thought I would like to have someone to talk to." She sat down on the side of the bed and drew the book from under the pillow. "Goodness! Where did you get this? I have not seen such a voluptuous dustcover since I have been in England."

"Are you going to tell her?"

"Why should I? What you read is no concern of mine. This nonsense won't hurt you, anyway."

"How do you know it's nonsense? Have you read it?"

"No, but it seems to follow the usual pattern—rich suitor, poor heroine dazzled by wealth, and somewhere, I suppose, a clean-limbed young hero to round everything off neatly."

"Is that why you married my father?" asked Fay. "Because he was a rich suitor and you were dazzled by his wealth?"

Miranda laughed. "What extraordinary notions you have about your father," she said, shutting up the book and returning it to its hiding place under the pillow.

"Adam is a cruel man," his daughter remarked.

"What nonsense!" Miranda was startled in spite of herself.

"Oh, no, it isn't," the child said with an air of conviction. "When you've lived in this house a little while, you'll see. You don't like the house, do you?"

"Well, I have only been here two days, and the weather has been depressing," Miranda answered evasively.

"That's right. The weather's always depressing here. Why don't you go away?"

"Why do you want to get rid of me?" Miranda retorted.

"Adam is not for you," said Fay, like a character out of her novel.

Miranda looked at the strange, lovely little face so like the beautiful face of the portrait, and suddenly she felt sorry for the child. It was natural, after all, that having been shut away with grown-up people for so long, she should be possessive about her father.

"You are very fond of your father, aren't you?" she said gently.

She felt she had been slapped when Fay replied with dispassionate calm, "No, I hate him—and he hates me."

"Oh, Fay, really! Your father may not be able to be with you very much, but he is continually thinking of your welfare."

"Is he?" said Fay, and her smile was unchildlike and rather disturbing.

Miranda felt a shiver run down her spine. To change the subject she said idly, observing the second bed in the room, "Do you not sleep alone yet at your age?"

"No," Fay answered indifferently. "Simmy sleeps with me. I have bad dreams sometimes."

"I see. Well, I think this side of the house is depressing anyway, and it is so far away from everyone else, isn't it? I found a room in the south corridor that must have been a nursery once, Fay—a big, sunny room with painted cupboards and pictures of animals. Was it ever yours?"

"Yes," the child said tonelessly, "but I'm not allowed to go in it now."

"Why not? It would make a much nicer schoolroom than your present one, and you would be next door to your father's room."

"That was the reason they changed it. Adam couldn't bear me close."

"Fay, dear, I'm sure that was not the reason," Miranda said.

But the child cried wildly, "It was, it was, it was! Ask Simmy—she'll tell you it's true!"

"Ask me what?" said Miss Simms's cool voice from the doorway. "What are you getting so excited about, Fay? You should have been asleep an hour ago. Do you want to have one of your nightmares? Really, Mrs. Chantry, this is most unwise. I would prefer it if in future you would say good-night to Fay before I've settled her for the night. What do you want Mrs. Chantry to ask me, dear?"

The brilliance had died out in the child's eyes and she looked sullen.

"Nothing," she said, darting a quick look at Miranda.

"That's not what I heard as I came in," Simmy said playfully. "Perhaps Mrs. Chantry can tell me."

"It was nothing of any importance," said Miranda lightly, and saw the governess compress her lips.

"In that case," she said, "perhaps you would be good enough to leave us now. It's time Fay settled down."

Miranda was beginning to dislike the governess and was not at all sure that such a woman was the ideal companion for a difficult, imaginative child. Simmy's discipline was clearly excellent, as no doubt, was her integrity. But Miranda found her depressing. There was too much altogether that was depressing about Wintersbride, Miranda thought.

The clock over the mantelpiece chimed the half hour and Miranda glanced at it wearily. Only half-past nine. But she might as well go to bed.

In her own room she smiled as she fingered the monogramed brushes on the dressing table. Strange, unpredictable man, she thought, to be so casual in his relationship with her, yet to remember so intimate a wedding present, and she traced the entwined initials M.C. on the back of the hand mirror with tender fingers, and remembered she had not thanked him.

THE FOLLOWING DAY the weather was little better. The fog had lifted, but the sky was still gray and overcast and rain clouds were gathering again over the distant tors.

"I had better not dawdle this morning," Miranda said to Nancy when she brought her breakfast in the morning. You can tell Mrs. Yeo I will see her at ten o'clock."

Nancy giggled.

"That'll drive her mazed," she said with enjoyment. "Not in her blacks this morning, she isn't, and not expecting to be sent for again."

But Mrs. Yeo was in her blacks by the time Miranda was ready for her, and they went through the same farce of ordering the menu for the day.

"Mrs. Yeo, the key is missing from the drawing-room door," Miranda said at the end of the interview. "Kindly see that it is put back without delay. It is not, I think, the province of Miss Simms to lock up rooms."

"Very good, madam."

Miranda made a face at the woman's retreating back. If it was going to be a struggle for supremacy at Wintersbride she was certainly not going to give way to Mrs. Yeo and her veiled insolence.

The uniformity of the ground-floor rooms began to worry her, and she amused herself for the rest of the morning shifting the furniture around and altering the positions of things. The luncheon gong caught her unprepared and Fay and Miss Simms were already coming down the stairs as she dragged a small oak settle to the other side of the hall.

"What are you doing?" asked Fay instantly. "That settle's stood under the window ever since I can remember."

"Well, it is nice to have change, don't you think?" Miranda said, and then took the child by the hand. "Look what I have done in this room—and in this one. Do you not think it looks better—more lived in?" coaxed Miranda.

"No," said Fay, "I don't like changes."

Miss Simms, standing behind her in the doorway, remarked gently, "Does Mr. Chantry approve of this?"

"Is there any reason why he should disapprove, Miss Simms?"

"No." The governess merely sounded thoughtful. "It's only that Fay's mother never altered anything and gentlemen are such creatures of habit, don't you think?"

It was the most delicate hint that she had been presumptuous and Miranda felt herself of flushing.

"Habits can be bad as well as good," she said shortly, and Miss Simms raised her eyebrows at such an obvious truth.

"Oh, quite," she said. "But I think we are keeping lunch waiting."

Miranda ate her lunch, conscious that her hands were dirty and her frock crumpled and smeared with dust, and would not have been in the least surprised if Simmy had ordered her out of the room to tidy herself. She felt discouraged by their reception of her morning's efforts, and already she was beginning to

wonder if Adam might not be annoyed with the changes in his
well-ordered rooms.

She tried to find some subject that might interest Fay, but the
child seemed indifferent to the conversation and Miranda was
left with the governess's polite replies to her questions. Miss
Simms would always do her social duty but she was clearly used
to long periods of silence at mealtimes. Adam himself, Miranda
had early discovered, was not a talkative man at the table. She
supposed the habit must be catching and thought again that she
had never before known a house where the human voice was so
seldom heard.

"Will you take me for a walk when you have had your rest?"
she asked Fay as they rose to leave the dining room.

"Alone?" the child said on such a note of surprise that
Miranda laughed.

"Yes, alone. I shall not eat you," she replied.

"Fay meant that she is never allowed outside the grounds
without me," the governess remarked quietly.

"Not allowed out by herself at her age!" exclaimed Miranda.
"Are you afraid of her losing herself on the moor?"

"Me lose myself? I'm moorland bred!" said Fay with deri-
sion. "There's nowhere I couldn't take you on the moor, is
there, Simmy, is there?"

She seemed unnaturally excited compared with her apathy
through lunch, and Miranda said with more enthusiasm than she
felt for the project, "Well, take me this afternoon. We have
been cooped up in the house for two days and we cannot stay in
for ever because of the rain. Besides, I want to see the country."

"May I? May I?" The child turned to her governess eagerly,
her small face beautiful again in unexpected animation.

The governess's pale eyes rested on her face for a moment,
and the sallow skin seemed to tighten across her cheekbones.

"Yes," she said quietly, "I have no objection so long as you
keep to the roads. I rely on you implicitly, Mrs. Chantry, not
to go onto the moor."

The words had a slightly sinister ring as though they were

intended to convey a warning, and Miranda said, "Are you afraid of escaped convicts?"

Miss Simms smiled thinly.

"After so much rain the moor will be very wet and there is still a little mist hanging about," she said prosaically, and Miranda felt a little foolish.

"Yes, I see," she said. "Very well, we will keep to the roads. Come and give me a shout when you are ready to start, Fay. I will be in my room."

When Fay knocked on her door an hour later Miranda swung round on her dressing-table stool and held out a welcoming hand.

"Come along in, *chérie*," she said. "I will not be long getting ready."

Fay watched her as she pulled open drawers, but she said nothing. Only when Miranda picked up one of the monogramed brushes to do her hair did she ask in a voice of suppressed fury, "Why are you using that brush?"

Miranda looked in the mirror at the dark, sullen reflection that appeared over her shoulder.

"Because I want to brush my hair," she said reasonably.

"Haven't you a brush of your own?" demanded the child.

Miranda, accustomed by now to her sudden intensity over trivial matters, replied without surprise, "This is my brush. Look, everything matches. The brushes and mirror and the little trinket boxes. They were waiting for me when I arrived. Do you not think they are pretty?"

"They are none of them yours, none of them!" Fay cried. "They belonged to my mother—they've even got her initials— M.C. Mrs. Yeo says they were a wedding present from my father—you have no right to use them at all."

She began to cry, and Miranda experienced such a sharp pang of bitterness that the pain was almost physical. She sat there fingering the raised initials on the brush.

"What was your mother's name?" she asked slowly.

"Melisande."

She put down the brush with distaste, then looked up at the weeping child. "Do not cry, Fay," she said. "I will not use them again. This was your mother's room, I think. I expect someone just forgot to put her things away. Now, shall we go for our walk?"

But Fay darted away from her.

"I hate you . . . I don't want to go for a walk . . ." she cried; and ran out of the room, slamming the door behind her.

Miranda did not try to follow her. The child's cruelty was natural, but the cruelty of Adam's heedless omission struck deep by reason of its utter indifference. Had he so little sensibility, she wondered painfully, that he saw no need to explain that his thought had not been for her, but for that other one whose room she now occupied, whose bed she slept in? Did he not care that his intimate gifts to a woman he had once loved should be used so carelessly by another?

Her eyes came back to her own reflection and she was surprised to see tears in them.

Why should I mind, she demanded angrily of her stricken self in the mirror. *I am not romantic.*

But she did mind. It had not been entirely a matter of experience, this strange marriage of hers. She had acknowledged from the start Adam's unconscious attraction for her and she had not thought that the time might never come when he would demand something more of her.

It was late in the afternoon when she left her room. Miranda thought she would visit the drawing room and take another look at Melisande's portrait, but when she came downstairs the key was still missing from the lock and the furniture in the other rooms had been quietly restored to the old positions. She ran to the bell rope and pulled it violently. It was Simmy who unexpectedly came through a green baize door at the back of the hall to ask Miranda what she wanted.

"The servants are busy getting the tea. What did you want, Mrs. Chantry?" she said.

"The furniture . . ." Miranda said. "It has all been changed again. By whose orders, Miss Simms?"

The governess stood patiently just inside the door. The un-accustomed flush had faded and she looked at Miranda now with a tolerant smile.

"Now you mustn't blame the servants for carrying on as they are accustomed to, Mrs. Chantry," she said in the soothing tones she used with Fay. "Mr. Chantry is expected home any moment and he would not like to see the house looking upset."

"Then it was you—" began Miranda, but Miss Simms started to walk toward the stairs.

"Excuse me, please, but our tea will get cold. Bessie will be bringing yours in a moment," she said, and went on up the stairs with no further comment.

Miranda stood in the center of the hall and her temper rose with the tired exasperation of a much tried child, so that when Adam unexpectedly walked in at the front door it was both a relief and an invitation to unconsidered speech.

"Adam, it is intolerable!" she exclaimed, her hands gesticulating wildly. "They treat me like a child or a—an irresponsible person! Have I any part in your home or am I just a—a stray cat you rescued and fed and then forgot?"

CHAPTER FIVE

"DEAR ME!" Adam said, looking at her curiously. "What a very odd greeting. Because I have to be away from home doesn't mean I've forgotten you. You'll have to get used to my absences, you know."

She knew that his misunderstanding was deliberate but she was too angry to be warned that it was not the moment or the place for a scene.

"That is not the trouble," she cried. "I wish to know if I have any—any authority at all at Wintersbride."

"Not when you behave like Fay," he retorted coolly, and as Bessie, carrying the tea tray, pushed open the green baize door, he added, "I'll just have a wash, then I'll join you for tea."

Miranda wandered slowly into the small study and watched the girl set out the tea things. For a moment she was tempted to inquire who had been responsible for putting the rooms back to their original order, but she knew Bessie would look at her with indifference and refer her to Mrs. Yeo.

"Are Fay and Simmy not coming down?" Adam asked as he came into the room.

"Miss Simms asked to be excused, sir," Bessie said. "Miss Fay has had a little upset and Miss Simms thought it best to remain in the schoolroom."

"I see," said Adam, but he gave Miranda a quick look as he sat down, and when the door had closed on the girl, he remarked a little dryly, "That makes two of you, or have you just been upsetting each other?"

Miranda began to pour out the tea. Already her temper had

cooled, and she was aware that Adam was not going to be sympathetic to domestic disturbances.

"I upset Fay, yes," she said. "But it was really your fault."

"Oh? How was that?"

"You did not tell me about the brushes."

"The brushes?" He frowned impatiently.

"The brushes in my room—the dressing-table set. The initials were mine and I did not know they had belonged to your wife."

She spoke as if she did not claim that position for herself and his eyes rested on her with a thoughtful expression.

"I see," he said. "Yes, that was stupid of me. Did Fay object to your using them?"

"Yes, but that is natural, isn't it?"

"Not very. She can't remember her mother." It suddenly struck him that Miranda must have thought that he had bought the set for her and he frowned again.

"It seemed sensible to leave them where they were as you had so little of your own, but if you don't care for the set you can replace it with something else," he said.

She looked across at him and smiled.

"It is of no consequence," she said. "The set is very handsome and expensive-looking. I have my wooden brush to use. Will you have a sandwich, Adam?"

He took the sandwich and regarded her uneasily as he ate.

"I'm afraid, Miranda," he said in his driest voice, "the delicacy of the situation had never struck me. It hadn't occurred to me that sentimentality had any place in our—business arrangement."

She gave him a wide, composed look from under the thick lashes. It was a look he was coming to know and it had begun to disturb him.

"Of course not," she said. "Do not give it another thought. The mistake was entirely mine."

And what the devil do you mean by that, he wanted to ask, but instead he inquired why she had seemed so upset when he had walked into the house.

"Because here they treat me like a child," she answered.

"So you said. A child and an irresponsible person. Are you an irresponsible person, Miranda?"

"Certainly not. I only wanted to change around the furniture."

He looked amused.

"Well, why didn't you?"

"I did, but when I came downstairs it had all been put back again and the key had not been returned to the drawing-room door, although I have told Mrs. Yeo, who blames Miss Simms."

The amusement left his eyes.

"I didn't know it was locked," he said briefly. "But no one goes in there, except, I suppose, to clean."

"Would you object if I used the room?" she asked him directly.

His face was expressionless.

"No," he said. "I have no objection."

"Then would you please be good enough to give Mrs. Yeo— or Miss Simms—instructions? They pay no attention to me."

But his interest had gone.

"You and the staff must settle these matters between yourselves," he said. "I'm not concerned with how you rearrange the rooms so long as you leave my study alone, but if you take my advice, Miranda, you won't upset Mrs. Yeo."

"I do not want to upset anyone," Miranda replied, feeling that she was being reproved unjustly. "But Mrs. Yeo will not try to be agreeable and Miss Simms makes difficulties over the simplest things."

"Such as?"

"Almost anything to do with Fay. It was a favor to be allowed to go for a walk without her, and even then we must not go on the moor."

"I see." He sounded noncommittal, but his eyes were grave as he added, "Simmy may often sound pernickety and even unreasonable to you, Miranda, but always remember that she knows what she's doing. Will you bear that in mind in the future?''

She would have liked to talk to him about the nursery she had discovered in the south corridor and suggest that the child's schoolroom be moved, but he had not encouraged her opinion of his arrangements the other night and seemed to have a dislike of suggestions that might alter in any way the present routine of the house. She began to think that the tragedy of Melisande's death was no greater for Adam than it was for his child and wondered why, when he was prepared to remarry, for conventional reasons, he had not chosen Grace Latham long ago. It would have been such a far more suitable arrangement. But no, she reflected shrewdly, that would not have done for Adam. Grace was pliant, and willing, Miranda was sure, to play second fiddle to the first wife, but she would expect the normal fulfillment of marriage. Was Adam then temperamentally cold, or was he one of those rare individuals who, once having given his devotion to one woman, could not contemplate again any intimate relationship with another?

At last Adam got up and stretched. He said, ''I must go up and have a word with Simmy now, then I have some letters to write. I'll see you at dinner.''

''Are you going to say good-night to Fay?''

''No, I don't think so,'' he replied calmly. ''It's not an institution we've indulged in for a good many years.''

She gave him a surprised look.

''But all children like to be tucked in,'' she said.

''Do they? Fay is probably the exception,'' he remarked, and went out of the room.

Miranda sighed. She could not understand Adam's attitude toward his daughter. At times he seemed to behave as though Fay's absurd claim that he disliked her was true. Had there never, she wondered, been a closer relationship between them?

Miranda shivered as she sat listening to the rain driving against the windows. She had a mental picture of the house as she had first seen it rising out of the mist with its blind, shuttered

look . . . Wintersbride. . . . She switched on all the lights,
then drew the curtains, shutting out the gray sad evening that
made a mockery of summer.

THE BAD WEATHER PERSISTED. June was heralded in with weeping skies and the days alternated only between rain and fog.
Miranda found little to do with her time. She did not again try
her hand at rearranging the rooms, and although the key was
returned to the drawing-room door she had not the heart to
venture inside. After the first week she had abandoned her
morning interviews with Mrs. Yeo, having become weary of the
recurrent phrase, "The *first* Mrs. Chantry always preferred—"
or even, "Mrs. Chantry did not approve." It was natural,
Miranda supposed, that Mrs. Yeo should resent her. She had
ruled Adam's household for seven years without interference
and it was not to be expected that she would take kindly to a new
mistress. But the days were very empty, and Miranda's efforts
to get to know Adam's child met with little success. Sometimes
she would walk to the village with Fay and her governess, and
when it was too wet to go out she would visit them in the
schoolroom and suggest a game.

Miranda saw little of Adam at this time. An emergency
operation took him into Somerset for a couple of nights and he
frequently stayed in Plymouth when his appointments were
booked late in the afternoon. He had prescribed early nights for
Miranda and there was little choice except to obey him and go to
bed at half-past nine. One could not read all day, she thought,
and there was nothing domestic with which to occupy herself.

Sometimes Miss Simms would come down after Fay was
in bed and sit with her until dinner time.

Mrs. Latham gave her promised dinner party at the end of
June, and Miranda went up to dress for it with a slight feeling of
trepidation. This was the first time she was to fulfill the terms of
Adam's bargain and she was anxious that his friends should
approve of her. She was uncertain as to what she was expected
to wear for a rather more formal evening in the country, and on

hearing Adam moving about in his room, she called to him to come and help her choose.

"What is it?" he said, sounding surprised. He had never before been into her bedroom.

"Please come in," she called. "I am having difficulties."

"Very well," he replied. "Open the door."

"It isn't locked," she shouted back, and he turned the handle and came in.

"Are you always as trusting as this?" he remarked with a little ironical twist to his mouth.

"As trusting as what?" she asked, her head in a cupboard; then, as she emerged abruptly and looked from his raised eyebrows to the open door between their rooms, she felt herself flushing.

"No," she replied sedately. "But in this case it is different, isn't it? The door has never been locked."

"Hmm," he observed, and stood looking at her with a speculative eye. She wore some brief undergarment that revealed more than it concealed and he crossed the room slowly and placed his hands on her narrow hipbones.

She stood very still, and for a moment she thought he was going to draw her into his arms. She looked up at his dark face and each line was suddenly familiar, and she felt an aching tenderness toward him as she waited.

But his eyes became coolly professional once more and all he said was, "You're still much too thin."

"Yes, Adam," she said, and wriggled out of his grasp.

"Well, now, what are the difficulties?" he asked her, and she plunged once more into the cupboard, pulling out dresses and tossing them at him in great haste.

"Well," he said, looking at her over the armful of clothes with a rather odd expression, "I'm not very used to acting as a lady's maid, you know."

"But it is only to choose for me," she said seriously. "I do not know if it is correct to wear the décolletage—" her hands began to sketch gestures "—or the high neck or the sleeves."

"Definitely not the décolletage," he said, looking amused. "A modest dinner dress is what is required. What about this? White is very suitable for the bride's first appearance, don't you think?"

She looked at the frock doubtfully. It was a charming creation, but she felt a little uncertain of Adam when he made remarks of this kind.

"If you think so," she said, and he tossed the rest of the dresses on to a chair.

"I definitely think so," he replied, and went back to his room.

GRACE AND HER MOTHER lived in an old, converted farmhouse on the other side of Shaptavy, and entering Mrs. Latham's low-ceilinged drawing room with its bright chintzes and old-fashioned Dresden china bric-a-brac, Miranda thought how much pleasanter it was than Wintersbride. The room seemed full of people and she experienced a moment of acute shyness as she stood beside Adam, acknowledging introductions. They regarded her with polite curiosity, these men and women who had been invited to meet her.

As the evening progressed, Adam glanced several times at Miranda with eyes that were amused and a little surprised. She was holding her own nicely with Stokes, who had a dry wit and a poor opinion of female intelligence, and old Benyon was clearly very taken with her. The women, too, had dropped their earlier reserve and complimented him on his young bride, and even Mrs. Latham, though she could not have been best pleased at the end of her daughter's hopes, remarked a little acidly, "An attractive young creature, my dear Adam, and nice manners in an age of a deplorable lack of them in the young, don't you think? But that's the French upbringing, I expect."

Adam grinned; he was not surprised that she was a success. There was no trace now of the shabby little waif he had rescued and married on such a curious impulse, and he realized that she was both attractive and unusual and that not one of the men present tonight would have believed or understood the terms of his marriage.

He turned to speak to Grace, aware that she had been watching him for some time.

"It was kind of you and your mother to help launch Miranda so successfully," he said quickly, and she smiled.

"But of course we did it for you, Adam. She is such a child and it can't be easy to become the wife of an important man when one has little or no experience."

"She seems to be doing all right," said Adam a little dryly. "And you've always overrated my importance, Grace."

She smiled again, but her eyes were less amused.

"Do you think so? Well, I hope you're going to be very happy, Adam. You know that's all I've ever wished for you."

"Yes, I know," he said, admiring the poise with which she hid whatever she might once have felt for him. "You're looking very well tonight. It's time, you know, you emulated my example and got married. There must be many poor devils who have been living in hopes for too long."

She winced. How clumsy men were, even the cleverest of them, she thought with a little spurt of anger. Was it possible that he had never really known what she had felt for him? His hasty marriage had come as a shock to her, but his choice of a wife had wounded her more bitterly. Adam Chantry, the cool, the levelheaded, to be caught by a pretty little gamine young enough to be his daughter . . . .

"You mustn't be like all bridegrooms and try to harry your friends into the married state," she said lightly. "There are still men and women who prefer the blessings of being single, you know."

Miranda was talking to Dr. Tregellis. He was, he had told her, the doctor practicing in the neighborhood; he attended everyone in the village and Wintersbride had been on his visiting list ever since Adam had first bought it ten years ago.

"Oh," said Miranda, betrayed into surprise, "then Fay was not born there?"

"No," said Dr. Tregellis. "If she had been I would certainly have brought her into the world. But didn't you know the child was born when Adam was practicing in London?"

"No," she said, "I did not know he had ever practiced in London. I thought he had always been here at Wintersbride."

"Oh, dear me, no," Tregellis said, looking at her rather curiously. "He had been married three years when he came down here. The child was two. He'd have been in Harley Street by now had he stayed, but it's the west country's gain. Your husband is a very brilliant surgeon, Mrs. Chantry."

"Yes," said Miranda, wondering why Adam had abandoned London for Plymouth. "I thought, somehow . . . ." She laughed a little awkwardly, aware that he must think it odd that she knew so little of her husband's affairs. "I thought, perhaps, Wintersbride was the family home."

"Oh, dear me, no," the doctor said again. "He bought the place as it stood, lock, stock and barrel. Old Colonel Hunter, the original owner, moved out, the Chantrys moved in and hardly a stick of furniture had to be altered."

That, then, thought Miranda, explained the curious impersonality of all the rooms, but how had *she* liked it—Melisande, with the flair for beauty that her drawing room betrayed?

"One forgets how time passes," Tregellis was saying with faint surprise. "It seems only the other day that the Chantrys moved into Wintersbride, and Mrs. Chantry's beauty was a nine days' wonder. People used to look through the gates, you know, hoping to get a glimpse of her in the garden." For a moment his eyes were introspective and a little sad, then he added rather hastily, "But that's all past history for you. You must have been a babe in arms at the time."

"I was nine," said Miranda.

"Did you attend Mrs. Chantry?" she asked, more for something to say than because she was curious.

"Yes," he replied, looking at her rather hard. "Poor soul, what a tragedy, but it was no one's fault in the end—no one's, you understand. Miss Simms blamed herself bitterly, but she had no cause to."

"But I thought Fay had been sent away all the time her mother was ill. Wasn't Simmy with her?"

"Oh, dear me, no. The child was with Nanny. Miss Simms was Mrs. Chantry's nurse-companion, you know. She only became Fay's governess afterward. But surely your husband has told you all this?"

"It was so long ago," she said evasively. "I think Adam feels that his first marriage has nothing to do with his second."

She began to dislike the little doctor's probing, bulging gaze and felt uncomfortable when he said with bluff heartiness, "Perhaps I've been talking too much, but meeting you was bound to revive old memories, you know, and Melisande Chantry was the most beautiful woman I ever saw."

Miranda was saved from a reply by Grace, who sent the doctor to talk to her mother and sat down herself in his place. Grateful for the interruption and anxious to please Grace, who she really thought was looking very handsome, she began to admire the sapphire pendant that looked so beautiful against her white skin.

"It was left me by a great-aunt," Grace said idly. "Incidentally, you never wear jewelery, do you Miranda? I haven't even seen your engagement ring. What did Adam give you?"

Miranda sat twisting the plain wedding ring round her finger, trying to think of an answer. Grace repeated her question and two of the other women broke off a conversation to discuss the more interesting subject of jewelery.

"Well, I . . ." Miranda began nervously.

Then Adam's voice said firmly behind her, "We had to send the ring back for the setting to be looked at. A stone was loose."

"Oh, what a shame," sympathized one of the women. "What is it like, Mrs. Chantry?"

"Diamonds," said Adam promptly. "I was conventional, I'm afraid, Mrs. Stokes."

"It's beautiful," Miranda said, relief making her unwary. "A square solitaire with—with baguette diamonds on each side."

"It sounds lovely—and expensive," gushed Mrs. Stokes,

and Miranda became aware of Adam's ironical eyes on her.

"Yes," he said dryly, "doesn't it?"

He took her home very soon afterward, and sitting beside him in the car, she gave a sigh of relief. She had enjoyed her evening, but there had been one or two awkward moments for which she had not been prepared.

"Did I—was I—well conducted?" she asked with that odd little formality of expression that she was apt to use when she was nervous.

"Very well conducted," he replied with a smile. "In fact, Miranda, you were a distinct success. Everyone thought you charming."

"And you, Adam," she said boldly into the darkness, "you did not find me charming?"

"I didn't say so," he replied, and there was a teasing note in his voice.

He heard her sigh and placed a hand for a moment over one of hers.

"I found you very charming, my dear," he said gently. "Do you want me to say I was proud of you?"

"That gives me great pleasure if you mean it," she said, flushing in the darkness, and moved a little closer to him. "Thank you for rescuing me over the ring, Adam. I could not think of what to say, and everyone was staring."

"Well, it's a pity your resourcefulness didn't desert you for a bit longer," he remarked with his old dryness. "You always have to embellish a story, don't you, Miranda? A square solitaire with baguettes on each side—a most exact description. Cartier probably won't have such a thing in stock."

"Cartier? Oh, but Adam, you don't have to be so literal. No one will notice now if I don't have a ring."

"Of course you must have a ring. You should have reminded me that it was part of the conventions. I shall write to Cartier's tomorrow."

She was silent, not knowing whether he was annoyed or amused or a little of both, and he suddenly put a hand on her knee.

"I'm not quite so thoughtless or so ungenerous as you must think me," he said unexpectedly. "There's some good jewelery in my safe, but after my—*bêtise* over the dressing-table set, I hesitated to offer it to you."

Melisande's jewels . . . . But Miranda had never known her, and all jewels, unless they were new, had been worn by someone else at some time or other.

"Thank you, Adam," she said gently. "If you do not mind, why should I? But I do not want to—trespass."

"What a nice child you are," he said, and turned for a moment to look at the fair, curled head so near his shoulder.

"Adam, I am not a child," she said. But they had reached Wintersbride now, and he laughed as he got out to open the gates.

"Aren't you?" he said. "Didn't you hear what old Benyon said, and Tregellis and the others?"

The house confronted them in the thin drizzle, blind and shuttered as usual. The pleasure Miranda had been feeling during the evening died as she entered the silent hall.

"Good night, Adam," she said, and would have gone upstairs, but he unexpectedly put a hand under her chin, tilting her face up for closer observation.

She looked up at him, aware that this time his interest was not wholly professional.

"Am I forgiven for hurting you over that dressing-set?" he asked.

She had not expected the question and for a moment she did not know how to answer. But as he gravely waited, searching her face with eyes that were curiously anxious, she replied gently, "It was not your fault that I was hurt. You had given me no reason to—misunderstand your actions."

He gave her a long look.

"Well, I've ordered another set for you from Asprey. Fay can have her mother's when she's older. Now go to bed and get a good night's sleep."

He did not wait for her stammered thanks but turned his whole attention to locking up the house.

CHAPTER SIX

THERE WAS ANOTHER WEEK of wet weather. Then, toward the end of June, summer suddenly came to the moor. It became so hot that the wild ponies sought shelter in the lanes, and at night Miranda could hear them outside the gates, their unshod hooves ringing in the stillness as they made off down the road.

Sometimes she would explore the moor in the cool of the evening, and once she got up very early to watch the sun rise behind the hut circles on Spiney Down. Adam met her in the hall as she slipped into the house, and his eyebrows rose.

"Hello, you're up early," he remarked, observing with surprise her bare feet and the sandals swinging from one hand.

"Yes," she laughed. "I've been on the moor. I have watched the sun rise over Spiney Down and I am very hungry."

"Hmm," he said noncommittally. "Well, you'd better join me for breakfast. It's all ready."

She was conscious that he was watching her as she ate, his eyes a little amused. She thought he looked very distinguished in his professional black coat and impeccable linen, distinguished but a little alarming. In the strong morning light the gray in his neatly brushed hair was very evident, and his dark face, fresh from his recent shave, already wore an air of the shrewd, observant consultant. She was unsurprised when he said with crisp approval, "You look better. A little too fine-drawn still, but healthier. Do you sleep well?"

"Very well, thank you," she replied meekly, then her mouth suddenly curled up in a grin. "You are very professional, Adam. Do your patients dare to confide in you?"

"Not more than is necessary for a diagnosis if I can help it," he retorted.

"I think, perhaps, you intimidate your patients."

"You do, do you? But I don't intimidate you, Miranda?"

Did he intimidate her? Yes, she thought, at times, when he looked at her as if she were a temperature chart with which he was not entirely satisfied. She wondered whether she should tell him this, but in the end she only replied a little smugly, "I am not a patient."

He replied with severity, "Oh, yes, you are, young woman. That heart of yours isn't all I should like it to be yet, so not so much of this sunrise watching, please, and more rest in your perfectly good bed—and keep your shoes on."

"Yes, Mr. Chantry," she said, and he laughed.

"You know—" he stirred his coffee idly, desiring unexpectedly to linger over the conversation "—I think I should have adopted you instead of married you."

"Why?"

"Well, look at you, with your scratched legs and your hair curling like a lamb's back! And that rather disreputable cotton dress never came out of Dubonnet's collection, I'll swear."

She looked surprised. It was so seldom that he appeared to notice what she wore.

"I got it in Plymouth for twenty-five shillings. It saves my grand ones," she told him. "Don't you like it?"

"Yes, the color suits you well enough, but you can always get things sent down from Bruton Street on approval, you know."

"Very likely," replied Miranda severely. "But you should not discourage me from saving your money, Adam. In France women are taught to be thrifty with their husbands' incomes."

"Indeed!" he said gravely. "Very praiseworthy, I've no doubt. Well, at least I've broken one French habit of yours of which I don't approve."

She looked a little alarmed. "What?" she asked, searching in her mind for French habits of which the British would not approve.

"You eat a decent English breakfast now instead of that continental nonsense," he said, and she giggled.

"Oh, Adam, what a funny thing to take so seriously. Wouldn't it—" she leaned across the table, coaxing him like a child "—would it not be nice if in this hot weather we had our breakfast on the terrace? In the south of France we had all our meals out of doors, my father and I."

There was nostalgia in her voice, and for a moment he experienced a brief curiosity about that other life of hers into which he had inquired so little, but breakfast on the terrace with Miranda distracting his thoughts from their well-ordered channels—no.

"Not at all nice, I'm afraid, Miranda," he said briskly. "I've no time to dally in the mornings and I dislike eating my food out of doors." He glanced at his watch and got up from the table. "Well, this won't do. I'm a quarter of an hour late as it is. Bidder will be waiting."

There were no more surprise breakfast parties and he did not catch her again for some time in her cheap cotton dresses and no shoes on her feet. By the time he came back in the evenings she had already changed into one of the expensive dresses from Dubonnet's, and with the dress went her party manners. She spoke when she felt she was expected to, sensing very quickly when he was tired or merely uncommunicative. Sometimes they would drink their coffee on the terrace, but it was the nearest Miranda ever got to the alfresco meals she had planned when the warm weather came.

Even Fay and Miss Simms seemed to share Adam's dislike of any departure from routine except for picnics. When Adam could dispense with the car, Bidder would drive them to Spiney Down or Ram's Tor, where there was a cave and a famous view from the top, or even farther afield to a point where they could glimpse the sea. Then he would leave them with their rugs and their picnic baskets and return for them in exactly two hours. On these occasions Miranda and Fay were unexpectedly united, for both disliked the expeditions and both were irked by the governess's unobtrusive supervision. Miss Simms did not appear to be watching them as she sat stiffly with her back against a boulder, reading or crocheting, but if they wandered out of sight she would call them back. Once, Miranda pretended not to hear and, taking the child's hand, pulled her down to hide in the bracken. Simmy, when she eventually found them, was very angry indeed.

"You should know better, Mrs. Chantry, than to play tricks like that," she said.

"But there is no harm in hiding," Miranda said reasonably. "I often used to hide from my nurse when I was small."

"You are not a child now," the governess retorted.

Miranda replied a little sharply, for the woman's attitude struck her as ridiculous, "Fay is a child, or should be. If you allowed her a little more freedom, Miss Simms, she might react more like a normal little girl."

Miss Simms's lips tightened at these last words and she glanced quickly at Fay, who gazed with interest at Miranda and remarked with complacency, "But I'm not normal, Miranda. I once heard Adam tell Grace I was not a normal child."

"You're talking nonsense, my dear," said Simmy briskly. "You never heard your father say any such thing."

"Oh, yes, I did. What does not normal mean?"

"It means not being like other people, so you see you could not have heard quite right."

"But I'm not like other people," said Fay proudly. "I don't want to be. I want to be different so that everyone will remember me like they do my mother."

"Now that's quite enough of this foolish talk," Miss Simms said quickly, and gave Miranda a warning look.

"Mrs. Chantry," the governess said as soon as the child was out of hearing range, "I must ask you not to make remarks of that kind in front of Fay, suggesting that I am responsible for her—bad behavior."

"Well, I think you are, without meaning to be," said Miranda candidly. It was time Simmy realized that Miranda also was not twelve years old.

They were walking back to their picnic spot, and for a moment Miss Simms paused.

"You don't understand," she said quite quietly, and did not look at Miranda as she spoke. "I realize that to you my methods may often seem old-fashioned and unnecessary, but believe me, I know what's best for Fay."

"I wonder if you do," said Miranda slowly. "Sometimes I think that you—and her father, too—do not treat her enough like an ordinary little girl."

"That's a matter you must take up with Mr. Chantry," the governess replied in her colorless voice, and said no more until they were in the car.

BUT IT WAS ADAM who took the matter up with Miranda after dinner that night.

"I wish, Miranda," he said without preamble, "you'd try to cooperate a little more with Simmy. It doesn't make her position easier, you know."

"Does Simmy," asked Miranda with a flash of temper, "have to report every trivial happening of the day?"

He studied her thoughtfully.

"No," he said, dropping his impatience, "only what she considers necessary. She thought, as you had given her the impression that in your opinion both she and I were at fault in our dealings with Fay, it would be as well if I had a talk with you."

Miranda felt herself flushing.

"But, Adam, it is all so silly," she said. "First she is annoyed because we hide in the bracken and then she is annoyed because I suggest—quite without rudeness, you understand—that Fay would behave more like a normal child if she was treated as such. She makes such unnecessary significances out of the most ordinary happenings."

He did not make any comment for a moment. Then he said quietly, "Well, I think it's unwise to put ideas into a child's head. You will agree that the minute you suggested she was not a normal child she promptly agreed with you and further expressed the opinion that she had no wish to be. Fay is very suggestible, you know. We all have to be careful.''

"Well," said Miranda, feeling uneasy at his consulting-room manner, "if she really did hear you tell Grace Latham that she was not normal, the idea was there already, wasn't it?''

"Yes," he said gravely. "It was a pity she heard that. One talks too loosely these days about normality and other claptrap definitions.''

"*You* wouldn't," Miranda said shrewdly. "Adam—she is not normal, is she?''

But he was not prepared to answer that question with such directness. "For heaven's sake, what is normality?'' he exclaimed. "Are you normal? Am I normal? Don't we all differ in varying degrees from the accepted pattern? Yes, Miranda, judged by the average third-form standard of giggling, basketball-playing little girls, Fay is not normal. But that doesn't make her a psychopathic case.''

"No, of course not," she said, and hesitated. Was this the moment to say what had been in her mind ever since she had come to Wintersbride?

"I'm sorry," she began, "if I have made things difficult for Miss Simms—or for you. But Adam, you are a doctor—does the trouble not go deeper?''

"What do you mean?" His voice was sharp.

"I only meant that you do not seem very fond of her," she said gently.

For a long minute he sat regarding her with a strange expression that held something of irony and something of sadness, too.

"Yes, my dear, that's true," he said with unexpected gentleness. "But you don't understand—how should you? Affection must be mutual. There are people who don't understand what is being offered and it's less exhausting to withdraw than beat perpetually on a locked door.''

She did not know what to reply. She was not really sure whether he was thinking of Fay's or his own inability to give when he spoke of affection.

Tears suddenly stung her eyelids and she jumped up and

turned toward the open window, seeking to escape to the garden. But he caught her hand as she brushed past his chair and held her beside him for a moment.

"Look at me," he said abruptly.

She turned her head unwillingly and the light from the reading lamp at his elbow slanted across her face, betraying the tears on her lashes.

"I've hurt you, haven't I?" he asked her gently. "You don't understand half the time what I'm trying to tell you."

She stood looking down at him, aware of the strong fingers on her wrist and the disconcerting scrutiny with which his dark eyes searched her face.

"If," she replied with dignity, "you are trying to tell me that you do not want my affection, you need have no fear I will embarrass you, Adam."

He sounded rather weary.

"No, I wasn't trying to tell you that. If you have acquired any—fondness for me, I can only be grateful, my dear, and humble, too. I don't think I can be a man who easily inspires affection."

"You!" she exclaimed, so quickly and in such a tone of disbelief that he gave her a surprised smile. "If you would only allow—"

She broke off warily at the look in his eyes and lowered her own when he said, "I seem to remember you once told me that it should not be difficult to make yourself love any man who was reasonably decent. Do you still think that?"

"Pierre used to say there is no such thing as love. It is only a matter of wishful thinking," she replied, and immediately sensed the change in him.

"Yes, well, I'm not particularly interested in Pierre's opinions," he said dryly. "And you, I think, would do better to stick to your own. I'm afraid we're an unsatisfactory couple, my daughter and I. You'll just have to make the best of us."

"Yes," she said, and gently withdrew her hand as she felt his fingers slacken on her wrist.

"That's a good child," he said absently, and reached for a book on the table beside him.

THEY WERE ASKED to dine out on several occasions by Adam's colleagues, but he was seldom was able to go. Miranda, if they accepted, went alone, and wondered which bored her most, the medical shoptalk that seemed to pervade most dinner conversations or the men who tried to flirt with her afterward.

"You've done your duty now," Adam told her with a smile at her disconsolate face when he packed her off for the last time without him. "Once we've returned hospitality, we can refuse all the rest. No one expects me to be social."

"We must have them here?" Miranda asked, looking a little alarmed.

"I think so. I've never entertained at Wintersbride, but you don't need to worry, Miranda. Mrs. Yeo will see to everything and she's an excellent cook."

He gave her a list of guests the next morning and, when she asked him blankly how the invitations should be worded, he said a little impatiently, "Call up Grace. She understands all that sort of thing."

Miranda was loath to display her ignorance to Grace, who was always so ready with advice. But it was important that she should not disgrace Adam, so she went to the telephone and asked the girl to lunch.

Grace was charming.

"But how sensible of you, Miranda," she said when she arrived. "You can't have much experience of this sort of thing, and I've played hostess for Adam before, you know."

"Here?" asked Miranda, acknowledging to herself that Grace would make an admirable hostess.

"No, not here. There's been no entertaining at Wintersbride since Melisande died, but occasionally Adam had to return hospitality to the wives of his various colleagues at some hotel. I used to help him out. Now, let me see your list, Miranda, and we'll decide on the table seating."

Grace took full charge. The order of precedence was explained to Miranda and the table decorations and arrangement of the rooms decided on. Grace interviewed Prout, the gardener, who was jealous of his fruit and flowers, and she made Miranda send for Mrs. Yeo in order to discuss the food. Mrs. Yeo did not appear to be pleased.

"A dinner party here?" she exclaimed. "There's been no entertaining here since that dinner my poor lady gave the year before she died. *You* remember, Miss Grace? That was a night!"

"Yes, Mrs. Yeo," Grace replied, giving her a level look. "This is not that kind of party at all. Mr. and Mrs. Chantry simply wish to return hospitality in as simple a manner as possible. I'm sure you'll do everything to make the evening a success."

"Certainly, miss, if you say so," the woman replied, ignoring Miranda from then onward. "Will you leave the menu to me, or do you wish to make suggestions?"

"Well, I think Mrs. Chantry would like to make a few suggestions," said Grace tactfully, but Miranda declined and Grace hastily made some suggestions of her own.

"You mustn't mind her, Miranda," she said a little apologetically when the housekeeper had gone. "She can be very difficult, I know, but she was devoted to Melisande and I'm afraid she resents a change. I must get Adam to talk to her. Now, Miranda, Adam will choose the wines, of course. I shall be here should you get into difficulties and I shall be over in the morning, of course, to do the flowers and make sure nothing's been forgotten."

Miranda was beginning to feel ruffled. She looked Grace straight in the eye and made her only bid for independence.

"I shall open up the drawing room," she said.

A faint flicker of negation passed over Grace's face but she said impassively, "Is it worth it for one evening?"

"It will not be for one evening once it is used again," Miranda replied. "Besides, the other rooms are not suitable. The women, anyway, will expect a drawing room."

"If it's weather like this the garden will be pleasant."

"But you cannot depend on the English weather."

"No, that's true. Very well, Miranda, but you had better let me explain to Mrs. Yeo. Adam will be sure to understand."

Miranda had been prepared for more argument on the subject, and she said a little defiantly, "Adam told me long ago that he did not object. It is Mrs. Yeo—and perhaps Miss Simms—who make the difficulties."

And you, she would have liked to add, but Grace only said with cheerful finality, "Well, that's all right then. I'll speak to Mrs. Yeo before I go."

It was not, after all, a very large dinner party. They would seat twelve for dinner. Miranda enjoyed the faint air of bustle the preparations lent to the house. It was heartening to see the impeccable Bessie forgetting small details for once, and even Grace, arranging the flowers and giving tactful orders to Mrs. Yeo, did not disturb her unduly. She sat on the stairs with Fay, who, pleased by the unusual break in her daily routine, seemed disposed to be friendly. Like a couple of children they watched the preparations.

"I wish I could stay up," Fay said, so like a normal little girl that Miranda warmed toward her.

"Simmy would never permit it, but I tell you what," she whispered. "If you can stay awake you can hide in the bend of the stairs; then, when the men have joined the ladies, I'll bring you a small glass of wine and we will toast each other, yes?"

The child's eyes were bright with excitement.

"Will you, really, Miranda?"

Just then Grace crossed the hall, a great sheaf of lupins and delphiniums in her arms.

"I'm ready to do the drawing room now, Miranda," she said. "Fay, you'd better go back to the schoolroom, out of everyone's way."

"No," she said, "I'm going to sit here and talk to Miranda."

"I'm afraid I need Miranda's help," Grace said calmly. "Run along up to Simmy, dear. You're not wanted down here."

Miranda felt the child stiffen with resentment at being snubbed and said softly, "Go—you will see it all tonight, remember?"

Without further protest, Fay unexpectedly kissed her and ran up the stairs.

"I'm glad to see," remarked Grace, turning toward the drawing room, "that you and Fay seem better friends. Adam will be pleased."

"The kiss was not a mark of affection," Miranda grinned. "It was a sign of her displeasure with you."

"What nonsense!" Grace sounded annoyed. "You know, my dear, I sometimes think you are the teeniest bit inclined to take too little trouble with Fay. A child's affection has to be won."

Miranda sighed. It was no good, she thought; she would never get on with Grace Latham.

"I will open the door for you," she said meekly. "There! It looks nice, doesn't it?"

Grace paused in the doorway for a moment and stood surveying the drawing room with eyes that held a hint of pain.

"Yes," she said slowly. "When Melisande was . . . ill, she spent all her time here."

"She could not walk up the stairs?" Miranda asked with sudden understanding. "She had her bed here?"

"No, she could walk upstairs," said Grace, her eyes fixed on the portrait, "but she liked to shut herself in here with her china and her objets d'art. Adam spent a mint on this room and it was a fit setting for her."

Miranda felt some of her own pleasure in the room's beauty diminish. In Grace's eyes the place had become a shrine, and in Adam's . . . ?

"We'd better get busy," she said briskly, and Grace smiled a little apologetically.

"Forgive me, Miranda," she said gently. "The room brings back memories, I'm afraid, but one mustn't be morbid, must one? Now, if you'll bring me the bowls and vases as I want them, I'll try to arrange the flowers."

Miranda, fetching and carrying for Grace, gave Melisande's portrait a rebellious look in passing. She was beginning to dislike this paragon whose legendary memory no one seemed able to forget.

"Not there," said Grace sharply as Miranda stood a great bowl of gladioli and scabiosa on an Empire escritoire. "That always goes on the pedestal in the corner. The *famille verte* for the escritoire—I have the roses ready."

"There!" she said when she had at last finished. "I hope you approve."

Miranda let her eyes travel slowly around the room, drinking in the glowing colors of the carefully chosen blooms, which, she had to admit, brought out all the more subtle tones of silk and china and delicately inlaid wood.

"It's beautiful," she said.

But her pleasure faded when Grace placed a bowl of crimson roses on the mantelpiece directly beneath the portrait, saying, "This is my own tribute. *Ena Harkness*. They were her favorites."

CHAPTER SEVEN

MIRANDA WENT UP early to dress. She wanted to lie for a long time in her bath and ponder upon her first dinner party in her own house.

As she thought of what she would wear, she wished a little sadly that Pierre could be there to see her in her finery and lend his own cheerful support to the ordeal. She had written to Michel who kept the inn at Ste. Giselle to inform him of her marriage and to ask for news of Pierre, but there was none. Monsieur Morel was still traveling, Michel had said in his reply, and the villa was sold. Should he return to Ste. Giselle, Michel would, of course, acquaint him with *mademoiselle*'s news and new address.

There was no discordance in the house. Fay had behaved admirably for the rest of the day. Miss Simms, although refusing to dine downstairs, had been gratified at being asked, and even Mrs. Yeo had accepted Miranda's congratulations on her choice of courses with a good grace. Adam had come home early after tea and brought with him her ring, which had come from Cartier's that morning. He had smiled when she had held out her hand and told him that he must put it on himself.

"How many women can say they received their wedding ring two months before they got the other, I wonder?" he had said, slipping it over her finger.

The ring had been made to order, after all—a square solitaire and two baguette diamonds, just as she had described.

"Is it two months already?"

"It is indeed. How time flies, doesn't it?"

He had seemed gayer, younger, as if for him, too, the evening was an occasion.

She chose the black dress with the bouffant skirt and the tightly boned bodice that had been Dubonnet's special pride. She had not worn it before and the fastenings were completely out of reach.

"Adam," she called, "come and hook me up."

It was quicker to call to him than to ring for Nancy and she was still twisting and wriggling in front of the mirror when he opened the door between their rooms.

She waited while he secured the last hook and eye, then wondered how many times he had performed this service for Melisande.

"There! Now let's have a look at you," he said, turning her around to face him. "Do I know this one?"

"No, I have never worn it—because of the décolletage, you know. But tonight is more formal, isn't it?"

"You and your décolletage! Black's too old for you, my child."

"Grace says—" Miranda's voice was solemn, but her nose was already wrinkling in mirth "—Grace says I am to try to remember I'm a married woman and that you have a position to maintain. So—we wear black."

He watched her turning and twisting in order that he should admire the dress. He had not allowed for these intimate interludes when he had suggested marriage to her, and not for the first time of late he experienced a sudden desire to pick her up in his arms.

"Grace isn't overblessed with much sense of humor, I'm afraid," he said, and Miranda pulled a face.

"She has a mind like a pudding—an English suet pudding," she stated. "Things sink into it and never come unstuck."

"Poor Grace!" He laughed, despite himself. "Still, you know, she's a good friend, and that counts for a lot."

"Umm . . . ." She did not want to discuss Grace and her

obvious good qualities. "But you *do* like my dress, don't you, Adam?"

"You look charming," he told her, his eyes suddenly serious.

"Oh, thank you. What is the time? I promised to show my dress to Fay."

He looked at his watch. "They won't be here for another twenty minutes or so. Wait one moment, I have something for you."

She was still preening herself before the long pier glass when he came back from his room and stood behind her.

"Will you wear these for me?" he asked, and clasped a small string of pearls about her neck.

She gazed, startled at their reflections in the mirror. His hands were on her bare shoulders and his eyes were curiously humble.

"They are beautiful," she said slowly. "Are they—are they from your safe?"

"Yes, but they've never been worn by anyone but my mother. I should like you to have them."

"Oh . . . ." For the first time she saw his mouth touched with tenderness. She turned with a soft little sigh and before she could stop herself had reached on tiptoe to kiss him. He regarded her with a rather strange expression but said nothing, and she spoke a little breathlessly.

"I'm sorry, but for that I had to thank you. But it commits you to nothing, Adam, I—it's—just that it's natural for me to kiss anyone when I'm pleased."

"Not anyone, I hope," he replied gravely and, stooping, kissed her gently on the lips.

There was just time to make her promised visit to Fay, and Miranda ran down the corridors, fleeing from Adam and from her own racing heart.

Miranda greeted her first guests without nervousness. Tonight Wintersbride was not hostile. It was as if for this one evening its air of secrecy had lifted and the silence, which had so oppressed her, was dispelled by the pleasant murmur of voices. If curious eyes turned to the portrait of Melisande more often than was quite polite, only Adam noticed it.

Adam, looking down the long table, tried to remember how many of them had been present at that other dinner party nearly nine years ago. Arthur Benyon, because Adam himself had insisted, and of course Grace. Tregellis, perhaps? No, she had considered the Tregellises bores and had not invited them, thereby mortally offending the pompous little doctor who admired her so much.

His eyes lost their look of brooding introspection as he watched Miranda at the other end of the table, so small, so very young to listen so solemnly to some dry-as-dust treatise on disease from her next-door neighbor. Well, the conventions were satisfied. After tonight they could return again to their isolation. It had, perhaps, been a mistake to break the rule of so many years.

Miranda shepherded the ladies to the drawing room and glanced up at the stairs as she passed. Yes, Fay was there. She could just discern a small figure in the shadows, peering out from behind the banister. The ladies had already drifted into groups. They were mostly elderly and Miranda listened with growing amazement as they discussed their servant troubles, their husbands' incomes and even his patients with lighthearted indiscretion. It was no wonder, she reflected, moving among them, that Adam never discussed his work with her.

Mrs. Stokes was looking at Melisande's portrait with frank curiosity.

"Was that the first wife?" she asked Grace in a penetrating whisper. "What a ravishing face! Very different from the present little thing, wasn't she? Surprising what men will marry *en secondes noces*. I've heard, my dear—"

Grace frowned a warning as Miranda joined them, and Mrs. Stokes, fluffy and far too girlish for her age, began to gush, "*Dear* Mrs. Chantry, such a wonderful dinner and how *clever* you've been with your flowers—*such* good taste."

"Oh, Grace did the flowers," said Miranda. "She really

organized the dinner, too. She has, as you said, excellent taste.''

Grace smiled and moved away, and Mrs. Stokes lowered her voice.

''Really? But isn't that rather odd, now that your husband has married again? You know, we all used to think—but perhaps I shouldn't be indiscreet.''

''Yes?'' said Miranda politely, but Mrs. Stokes gave a little trill of laughter and patted her tinted hair self-consciously.

''No, I really mustn't give away state secrets. There was evidently nothing in it as things have turned out, was there? Oh, I see you've got your ring back—do let me look. Goodness, that must have cost a fortune! What a lucky girl you are, my dear. The women have been chasing your husband for years, you know.''

It was a relief to see the men again. Miranda slipped out of the room as the conversation became general again, and ran back to the dining room.

Adam and old Arthur Benyon were still arguing about the efficacy of a new treatment for Parkinson's disease, and the specialist broke off to say, with a wave of his cigar, ''Ha! We are about to be admonished by your charming wife, Adam. She has come to tell us that the ladies are getting impatient.''

''No, no,'' laughed Miranda, pouring a little claret into a sherry glass. ''But I have a private date to keep.''

She carried the glass into the hall.

''Fay!'' she called softly. ''Come down, my rabbit. Here is your wine.''

Fay descended to the bottom stair.

''I thought they'd never come out,'' she said. ''The dresses aren't very chic, are they, Miranda?''

''No, but they would keep their best for grander occasions. Now—I will have a sip to toast you, and then you take a sip to toast me.'' She raised the glass. ''Here's to the beautiful Miss Chantry who cannot appear at the party because she would break too many hearts!''

Miranda took a sip of the wine, then handed the glass to Fay, who, delighted by such a conceit about herself, was about to put it to her lips when Adam's voice cut in, so sharply that they both jumped.

"Fay! What are you doing?"

"Drinking a toast to Miranda," the child replied, insolence already creeping into her brilliant eyes.

He took the glass from her so roughly that some of its contents spilled on Miranda's dress.

"How dare you give the child wine?" he demanded, rounding unexpectedly on Miranda. "Haven't you learned yet that I will not have my orders disregarded?"

"But, Adam," she protested, utterly bewildered, "it will not harm her. In France all children take wine as a matter of course. It was just a little treat—a novelty, you understand."

"We are not in France," he replied icily. "And if you can't be trusted not to teach Fay bad habits as soon as Simmy's back is turned, then you'd better keep away from her altogether."

The tears gathered on Miranda's lashes. She could not answer him when he spoke to her like this; she could only stand there, looking up at his white, angry face, while the hostility of the house settled about her once again.

Fay, frightened, had already turned and fled up the stairs, and Miranda's head drooped to hide her tears.

Arthur Benyon, who was standing behind Adam, cleared his throat.

"I think you should explain your attitude, Adam," he said quietly.

"There's nothing to explain," Adam replied. "Miranda will just have to get better acquainted with the rules of this house, that's all."

"She's your wife, remember—not one of your nurses who has broken a hospital rule."

There was a slight sharpness in the old man's voice and Adam controlled himself sufficiently to reply icily, "I apologize, Miranda. You're not to blame."

"I'm sorry," she whispered. "I—I must go and wipe my dress."

She lifted her full skirt with shaking fingers and ran away up the stairs.

IT WAS, surprisingly, Simmy who came to her room, offering to help. Miranda turned, prepared for indignant reproaches, but the governess only took the towel from her hand and, kneeling, began to rub the wet patch on her skirt with practiced fingers.

"Dear me, what a pity," she said. "Such a pretty dress. But the stain won't show when it's dry."

"I do not understand why he was so angry," Miranda said, the tears running unchecked down her white face. "Perhaps I should not have encouraged Fay to come down when she should have been in bed, but I cannot understand what harm there is in a small glass of wine."

"Mr. Chantry was probably upset," Miss Simms replied, not looking up. "Something of the kind happened when Nanny was with us."

"Such a storm in a teacup, and in front of Mr. Benyon, too."

"Mr. Benyon must have understood. He's known us all for a long time. There! I think that ought to do."

Miss Simms looked up and smiled, and Miranda received the strange impression that, like the house, Simmy did not always reveal her real personality.

"Simmy, help me," she said impulsively, unconsciously using the household's affectionate abbreviation of the name. "Sometimes there seems much I do not understand."

The governess got to her feet.

"I know," she said. "I've often wished I could help you, Mrs. Chantry. I've seen you look at me, thinking me fussy and old-maidish, and sometimes I've been tempted to give you a hint."

"A hint? But what is there to hint at?"

Miss Simms sighed.

"Perhaps nothing that would do any good, now. So much is past history, and no doubt Mr. Chantry thinks that need not concern you. You are—forgive me—so very young to bear other people's burdens."

Miranda's tears had stopped.

"There is, perhaps, some mystery about the first Mrs. Chantry's death?" she asked, trying to understand.

"No—no mystery. There was an accident," the governess answered, and turned away. "I've always blamed myself very much. That's why I am doubly careful with the child. I've always been deeply touched by Mr. Chantry's trust in me, after Nanny's behavior."

"What did Nanny do?" asked Miranda, and the governess's mouth pulled down a little at the corners.

"She was dismissed a year after Mrs. Chantry died. She was possessive, you know, like so many old nannies, and had a bad effect on the child. Other things came to light that need not concern you now, and she had to go."

"Whatever happened," Miranda said gently, "I am sure my husband's trust in you was always justified, Miss Simms."

For a moment the long, sallow face wrinkled with an emotion too long suppressed, and she said a little unsteadily, "Do call me Simmy like the rest of them, Mrs. Chantry, and—thank you for your understanding. Now—" her voice became firm again "—you will be missed downstairs. Dry your eyes and powder your nose and don't let them see you've been upset. Now I must go back to Fay and see that she gets off to sleep."

Miranda smiled. "Dear Simmy," she said, kissing her on the cheek, "I shall always come to you for counsel in future."

She joined her guests in the drawing room, saying dutifully to the first person she spoke to, "I spilled something on my dress. I had to go and dry it." But nobody had noticed her absence.

Adam seemed perfectly normal and was exerting his not inconsiderable charm on dull Mrs. Tregellis, who always had so little to say. He broke off his conversation to ask Miranda if she had had any coffee. When she replied that she did not want any, he said with his familiar raillery, "Not afraid of it keeping you awake at your age, are you, my dear? Well, I'll get you some brandy. It will do you good."

She took the brandy from him, but she would not let her eyes meet his. It seemed a long time ago that he had returned her kiss and looked at her as she had thought a man should look at a woman.

She stool alone for a moment beneath the portrait of Melisande, watching Adam while she let the big balloon glass revolve slowly between her hands.

"You mustn't look at your husband like that, Mrs. Chantry," remarked old Benyon beside her. "Your guests will think he beats you in private."

She looked up at him, laughing a little nervously.

"But how absurd! Adam would never beat anyone."

He stood looking down at her in silence for a moment, his fierce eyebrows twitching violently. Then he said, "You know, sometimes people act strangely because they suppress an emotion or a fear for too long."

"Yes?" If he was trying to explain Adam's disturbing behavior, Miranda thought, he was not being very clear.

"Has Adam never talked to you about his first marriage?" he asked.

"No, but that is not surprising," she answered gently. "Grace Latham has told me that he was very much in love with his first wife. I think he has not forgotten her."

He wondered if she realized how much she was admitting and for a moment he felt impatient with Adam. What right had he to marry a mere child and shut her away in this gloomy house if he was not in love with her?

"Well, perhaps I'm a cynical old bachelor," he replied gruffly. "But I've never believed in this love-of-a-lifetime business. A man can fall in love many times, and a woman, too. So much depends on the circumstances. But I expect at your age you think that's a most prosaic and unromantic point of view."

"Oh, no," said Miranda seriously. "I think it is very sensible. Me, I am not romantic."

"You're not?"

"Oh, no, I have the practical mind. In France they have the view that marriage should be sound first; then affection, love, what you will, should not be difficult."

"Really?" he observed slowly. "And did you tell Adam all this?"

"Of course—when he suggested that we marry. He would not have liked that I should be impractical. We understand each other very well."

"Good God!" the specialist exclaimed, and she looked uneasily at the expression on his face. She had said too much, as usual.

"I think perhaps I talk too much," she said, lowering her eyes. "You will please forget if I have been indiscreet."

He rubbed the side of his nose thoughtfully.

"On the contrary, you are a very remarkable young woman, you know, Miranda—do you mind if I call you Miranda? You're far too young and attractive for me to continue to address you so formally. You know, I think you will be very good for Adam."

"Do you think so?" she said. "He thinks I am still a child, you know."

"Yes, I know. He's probably very conscious of those nineteen years' difference, my dear."

"But you do not think me a child, Mr. Benyon, and there is much more than nineteen years' difference."

He smiled a little wryly.

"Very much more, but when one is old one's values alter. Age is so much a matter of mentality, don't you think? Your husband's a very lonely man, Miranda."

Her big eyes widened, and in that moment she was wholly childlike as she answered ingenuously, "Is he? I thought it was I who was lonely, for I have no one of my own, and he has Fay, even though he does not seem to be very fond of her."

He considered her thoughtfully, puffing on his half-finished cigar. Then he said, his eyes going to the portrait, "She's too like her mother. She must be an ever present reminder of things he would rather forget."

She shivered, and the old man said softly, "*You* needn't fear a ghost, Miranda. You are young and fresh and delightfully uninhibited. That's why I think you'll be good for Adam."

She looked away from the portrait and said slowly, "But you saw how he looked at me on the stairs—as if he could have struck me."

But Adam, Benyon knew, had not seen Miranda with his mind. He had been brutally reminded of that other dinner party so long ago, and he had seen only the child brought back into the house against his orders, standing on the long table in the candlelight while Melisande, beautiful, arrogant and excited by the laughter of her guests, held a goblet to the baby's lips.

"Well, you must do one of two things, my dear," he said briskly. "You must ask him for an explanation, or you must forget it completely. In either case you must forget it. I do assure you that little incident had nothing to do with you."

But she did not find it easy to ask Adam for an explanation. When their guests had gone he sent her to bed at once with the observation that she was looking much too tired and washed out. When she lingered, searching for words into which to put her question, he touched her cheek with gentle but restraining fingers.

"Your party was a great success, Miranda—thank you. And I want to apologize for that unforgivable little scene earlier. I should not have spoken to you as I did."

"Why were you so angry with me?" she asked.

"Believe me I was not angry with you—or only indirectly," he said, and his eyes were very weary. "You were not in any way to blame."

"Then can you not explain?"

"The fault lies in the past. It has nothing to do with you. Forget my rudeness if you can, and remember, if it means anything to you, you will always have my gratitude and admiration."

The rather formal phrasing had a chilly sound and she said with a shiver, "I do not think I want admiration or even gratitude. Both are cold things by themselves."

He smiled.

"Foolish child! Go to bed and to sleep and forget my clumsy attempts to make amends."

"Adam—" she said, instinctively reaching out a hand to him, but he only smiled again and turned away.

"Good night," he said. "And don't hurry up in the morning."

"Good night," she replied and went slowly up the stairs.

JULY WAS A DULL MONTH, Miranda thought, as the days went by and she was much alone. Sometimes she thought that Adam deliberately shut himself away from her. He was very busy and was beginning to look strained and overworked, but he would not yet accede to Arthur Benyon's suggestion that he take a holiday. To holiday abroad with Miranda and encounter the intimacies and snares of small, overcrowded hotels would be to court disaster. It was becoming increasingly plain to him as the weeks went by that the child no longer left him unmoved. But had he the right, he reflected wearily, to break the rules that he himself had laid down just because she might be generous and he, despite his earlier conviction, was still a man of natural appetites?

He was too tired mentally to do more than push the problem aside for the moment, but later he would have to get away.

It was beginning to worry him a little that he was obliged to leave her so much alone, but he was relieved that since the night of the dinner party Fay had appeared to have dropped her earlier hostility and, indeed, had veered the other way. He gave Miranda, however, one word of warning.

"Don't get too fond of her," he said. "Fay's affections are very capricious."

"Perhaps. But you see, Adam, she does not have to talk to me as a grown-up. That makes a difference."

He smiled.

"Yes, I rather hoped it might. Well, I'm delighted things are working out better, but don't trust Fay too far, my dear."

Her forehead wrinkled.

"Not trust her?" she repeated. "What a strange thing to say of your own child."

"Perhaps it is," he replied gravely, "but I know her rather

better than you do. You're a nice person, Miranda, and I wouldn't like you to be hurt.''

"I think," she said gently, "it is the ones who do not trust enough or give enough who get hurt.''

"You think I'm hard and undemonstrative with Fay, don't you, Miranda?" he said.

She smiled at him apologetically.

"I think, perhaps, you do not understand her very well.''

"I understand her only too well," he replied with a certain harshness, then his face softened as she turned her head away.

"Love her if you must," he said with gentleness. "Perhaps, after all, you're what she needs.''

But Simmy did not encourage intimacy between Miranda and the child. She only smiled a little secretly when the subject was mentioned and suggested that Miranda find herself some useful occupation.

"But I am not allowed to be useful," Miranda complained. "You would think, would you not, that in this big house there must be a place for me?''

"Yes, I'm afraid Wintersbride must seem lonely to you," Simmy said, busy with her crocheting. "You should get away more often and see people. Why not persuade Mr. Chantry to let you go up to London for a few days and do some shopping and go to a theater or two?''

Miranda looked surprised.

"But, Simmy, what should I do in London all by myself?''

"Have you no friends—girls of your own age whom you knew before your marriage?''

"No," said Miranda simply. "I was too busy earning my living where and how I could. My one friend, Pierre, is in Europe somewhere, and since my father died, I have lost touch, you understand?''

"Yes, I see. This friend you speak of—you were fond of him, perhaps?''

"Oh, yes. Pierre and I were brought up together. He is very cheerful—very charming. I owe much to Pierre.''

"Indeed?" The governess's eyes held a curious expression. "You must miss him. Does he not write to you?"

"There is no news of him yet for he travels still. But one day—yes, I will see him again."

"Then I should be careful, Mrs. Chantry," Simmy said, and added, as she saw Miranda's forehead wrinkle in perplexity, "I only meant that old friendships can be misunderstood, but I'm sure you realize that."

Miranda was a little puzzled by this conversation and later wondered if Simmy had spoken to Adam, for after dinner that night he asked her suddenly if she would care to go away for a few days.

"But where would I go?" she replied reasonably. "I'm afraid I have no friends of my own, Adam, and it would not be practical to waste your money in a hotel all by myself."

"Well, that's a very laudable attitude," he said with rather dry amusement. "But quite unnecessary, I assure you. I have quite a comfortable private income apart from what I earn, you know."

"Have you?" she said with polite interest. "I did not know."

"Well, run up to town and be extravagant," he said with a vague feeling that he had been neglecting her. "Buy yourself some fripperies and see the sights. Do you like the theater?"

"Oh, yes, but not alone. One should have someone with whom to laugh and cry."

"Well, then, take Grace, if you've no friends of your own."

Miranda looked at him under her lashes.

"I do not very much want to go away with Grace," she said. "Is it that you wish me to go away, Adam?"

"Not if you don't want to," he replied a little impatiently, "but Simmy seemed to think a change would do you good. I'm sorry you don't care more for Grace, Miranda. She's a bit old for you, perhaps, but she's been very kind and helpful since you came here, I must say."

"Yes," said Miranda dutifully. Had he really thought, then, that Grace would sulk and parade her disappointment for him and everyone else to see?

"You do not, I think, understand women very well," she said, and he looked suddenly tired.

"Perhaps you're right," he said shortly. "In fact, according to you, I understand very little—about my daughter, for example, and presumably about my young but critical wife."

"You are laughing at me, I hope? But, Adam—if you wish to make a return to Grace for her kindness to me, I will willingly go with her to London as you suggested."

He ruffled her fair head with a careless gesture.

"No, you conscientious goose," he laughed. "In any case it was your pleasure I was thinking of rather than hers. But if you prefer to stay with a rather neglectful and dull-witted husband, I shouldn't be anything else but flattered, should I?"

"Yes," she said with grave consideration which always amused him, "I think I would prefer to stay with you."

CHAPTER EIGHT

HE DID NOT SUGGEST again that Miranda should go away with Grace, but he tried himself to snatch a day off when he could and to devise some outing for her. Sometimes they would go to Torquay and have lunch at the Imperial and look at the shops.

Miranda was touched by his efforts to please her. She knew that he must begrudge the wasted hours, but when she suggested a simple outing nearer home he overruled her.

"You do not have to do this," she told him once. "We could take a picnic perhaps to Spiney Down or walk by the river and pick watercress, and you would not need to waste a whole day."

"Nonsense," he replied. "You need taking out of yourself."

Miranda sighed. To look at shops and eat expensive food you did not want was not being taken out of yourself, she thought with a certain despondence.

"You don't really much care for these expeditions, do you, Miranda?" he asked as they drove home.

"But yes, it is very kind of you to give up a day to—to look at shops," she protested quickly.

"Honest, now."

She lowered her eyes.

"Well, perhaps not very much. You see I do not want to buy anything."

He laughed.

"I thought all women liked window gazing," he said. "Well, we'll have to think of something else."

He was, she knew, relieved by the lifting of that particular obligation, but as July drew to a close and the hospital was short staffed with the commencement of the holiday rota, the picnics and other small relaxations somehow never materialized.

Seeing that his unavoidable preoccupation with other matters was beginning to worry him, Miranda tried to please him by asking Grace to the house and accepting invitations to lunch or tea. But she did not much enjoy these visits. Grace and her mother were both inclined to quote Melisande rather too often and Miranda had little to say that would interest either of them.

"I suppose," she said to Simmy after one of these visits, "I am unreasonable, but I do get so tired of hearing of the perfections of the first Mrs. Chantry."

Miss Simms regarded her dispassionately.

"Miss Latham was very devoted to her," she said. "She does not mean to make unflattering comparisons."

"But she does all the same, and so does Mrs. Yeo. Even you, Simmy, must think in your heart that I am a bad second choice."

Simmy's smile was a little enigmatic as she replied, "You should not be so fanciful, Mrs. Chantry."

Miranda sighed. She had not the qualities for the making of a *grande dame*, she thought with a regretful shrug; people did not respect her. But there seemed little she could do about it.

WITH THE BEGINNING OF AUGUST the hot weather returned. Day after day the sky was an unbroken arc of blue, meeting the shimmering horizon of the moor, and the River Scaw was a mere trickle of water under the old clapper bridge.

It was too hot, Simmy said, for picnics, but Miranda liked to wander by herself up the bed of the river to the shallow pools, which still held sufficient water, and look for watercress. She washed it from the stream in which it grew, and ate it on biscuits filched from the dining-room sideboard with the guilty knowledge that Adam would not approve.

She was sorry for Adam in his correct stiff collar, she reflected, as she lay on her back in the cool bracken, watching a lark soaring above her. She wondered if Adam would become a different person were he to idle in the sun, clad in a faded cotton shirt with no buttons. Would he speak then of the things he never told her or lie content at her side in the bracken while she tickled his nose with a stalk? But that she supposed was being fanciful and neither Simmy nor Adam would approve. She could not, anyway, imagine him divorced from his professional attire, and perhaps the transformation would not suit him. He was fastidious about his clothes, and even during weekends, when he inspected his garden, he still looked what he was—a distinguished professional man with little time for dalliance.

"And I," she said, indulging in her old habit of thinking aloud, "have too much time, and too little company." The French were right. Marriage should be taken seriously, and if there cannot be affection there can at least be children and the firm rock of mutual understanding. What thoughts, she reproved herself, for one who is scarcely a bride. But then she remembered the way Adam had looked at her when she had thoughtlessly kissed him on the night of the dinner party, and nodded her head gravely.

"He is not so cold as he likes to think, that one," she said.

The following day started badly. Adam had not come home the night before, and Miranda, whose custom it now was on these occasions to have a light supper brought to her on a tray, was in Mrs. Yeo's bad books.

"The master has given express orders that meals should be as usual when he's not here," she said in an aggrieved voice at the end of a list of small complaints.

"I cannot feel," said Miranda, trying to speak amiably, "that Mr. Chantry minds what I eat or where I eat it."

"If you will pardon me, madam," the housekeeper retorted, "the master was most insistent that I saw to it you have a proper dinner. Besides, it's bad for the maids. Bessie is getting slack."

"But, Mrs. Yeo," Miranda pleaded humorously, "why should I sit all alone in that dismal dining room for hours just to keep Bessie busy handing me dishes I do not want?"

"I'm sorry you find the dining room dismal, madam. In my *late* lady's time—" Mrs. Yeo began stiffly, but Miranda interrupted.

"Don't say it!" she cried. "Don't say it, Mrs. Yeo, or I shall scream!"

The woman, offended, left the room without another word, and Miranda chided herself for her impatience. But she was not feeling well. She had felt shivers along her spine ever since she had got up that morning and her head felt heavy. She supposed she must have caught a chill. Simmy, too, was not feeling well. She had a headache and announced her intention of lying down for the afternoon.

"When Fay has had her rest she can play in the garden," she said. "You'll keep an eye on her, Mrs. Chantry, won't you?"

Miranda did not at all want to keep an eye on Fay, but it was so seldom that Simmy ever claimed any time for herself that she agreed at once. They had tea in the garden by themselves, but Fay got stung by a wasp and by the time this mishap was dealt with they were both hot and cross and sticky with jam.

"What shall we do now?" Fay demanded when they had been indoors to wash.

"Oh, *chérie*, can you not amuse yourself for a little? I have a headache," Miranda said.

"That's just an excuse, like one of Simmy's," the child replied. "All grown-ups say they have a headache when they don't want to do something."

"But I really have—oh, well, what would you like to do?"

"Let's go up the lane and look for wild strawberries."

"You go and I'll stay quietly here."

Fay's eyes were reproachful.

"You know I'm not allowed outside the grounds alone," she said, and her lips trembled.

"Oh, very well, my cabbage, I'll come."

It always surprised her that Fay, so difficult in other ways, was obedient to rules that could so easily be broken without much harm. She had only to open the gates, which were never locked, and walk out, just as she had only to enter the forbidden rooms in the house, but she never did.

They poked about in the high, dusty banks for strawberries.

They did not find any, but Miranda picked up a young sparrow that was lying on the side of the road and stood looking down at the bird compassionately. Its eyes were already glazing, and although it fluttered its wings, it lay without protest in her hand.

"What is it?" Fay asked excitedly, slipping down from the bank. "What have you found, Miranda?"

"Look, a little bird. It is dying from the drought, I'm afraid. We will take it home and see if we can save it."

"Let me hold it," said Fay, and Miranda laid the sparrow carefully in the child's hands.

Fay stood looking down at it for a moment, her face curiously lovely with an unfamiliar expression of tenderness. Then, with a sudden, passionate gesture, she flung the bird into the bracken. The shock was so sudden, the change from one mood to another so startling, that before she could stop herself, Miranda had slapped the child across the face.

"Why did you do that?" she demanded, white with anger.

Fay began to cry.

"I didn't want you to have it," she sobbed. "It would have been yours, not mine, and you would have loved it more than me."

"That would not be difficult," retorted Miranda. "I cannot love a little girl who is wantonly cruel."

She picked up the bird, but it was dead, and she laid it gently back in the bracken.

"It would, perhaps, have died anyhow, but you have killed it," she said.

The child looked frightened.

"Don't tell Simmy, Miranda. I didn't mean to kill it."

"Didn't you?"

"No, no. You hit me, Miranda. Simmy's never hit me."

"What a pity," said Miranda coldly. "Go back to the house now, we are nearly at the gates. I am not coming in for a little while."

"Will you hate me now like Adam does?"

"Adam does not hate you, and I do not expect I shall, either. I should not have slapped you, Fay, but I think perhaps it has not hurt you. Now go back to the house. It must be nearly your bedtime.''

Fay's tears stopped. She looked at Miranda a little uncertainly, then, without protest, walked quietly back to the gates.

Miranda sat in the bracken beside the dead bird, feeling very sick. Her head was throbbing violently now, and the evening heat seemed to grow more intense. She sat there for a long time, unwilling to return to the house whose hostility seemed suddenly to menace her. Then the first roll of thunder in the distance sent her wearily to her feet.

It must have been later than she had supposed, for Adam had already returned and was coming down the driveway to meet her.

''What have you been doing with yourself?'' he asked as they met. He took a quick look at her face. ''You've got a temperature, and a pretty high one at that.''

He placed a hand on her forehead for a moment, then his fingers went automatically to her pulse, and she burst into tears.

''My dear child!'' he said and without further comment, picked her up and carried her into the house.

He carried her into his study and put her in his big leather chair, then opened the drawer in which he kept his thermometer.

''Why did she kill the bird?'' Miranda said.

He paused in the act of shaking down the thermometer to ask sharply, ''Who killed a bird?''

''Fay. It was dying of thirst, I think, and I was going to bring it home to make it well, and she threw it down and it was dead.''

He put the thermometer down on his desk and came and sat on the arm of her chair.

''You shouldn't have been out in all this heat when you weren't feeling well,'' he said, sounding unsurprised. He put an arm round her. ''You've had a shock, haven't you? Now perhaps you'll understand why I've never allowed Fay to keep animals. Years ago she had a kitten and Simmy had to get rid of it in—rather unhappy circumstances one time when I was away.''

"But why—why?"

"Jealousy—a form of misplaced affection. Did she think you were going to make a pet of the bird?"

"I don't know. She said she did not want me to have it because I would love it better than her."

"You see? I tried to warn you about Fay, Miranda, but I think you only thought I was hard and unfeeling. Her affections are unbalanced—she can't help it. Arthur says it's nothing to worry about, but we have to be careful."

"Mr. Benyon?"

"He's a nerve specialist, you remember. He's kept an eye on Fay ever since her mother died."

"Yes, I see. Why did you not tell me of this before? I would have understood you so much better."

"Would you? I suppose I should have explained about Fay when I asked you to marry me, but I didn't want you to get the idea that she was abnormal. She's not, you know. Just highly strung and badly adjusted at present. That's why I leave her to Simmy. Any efforts of mine to establish a normal relationship only upset her."

She heard the weariness in his voice and said gently, "You have tried to love her, I think. Did she hurt you, Adam?"

"Oh, yes," he replied a little bitterly, "I've had my day like everyone else. But I was the first to fall from grace, you see, and a child's lost affection takes a little getting used to."

At that moment he was no longer the coldly professional Adam Chantry concerned only with the fact that she had a temperature. He was the man who held her heart whether he wished it or not, the man who, despite his self-sufficiency, needed comfort as badly as did she herself. It seemed the most natural thing in the world to scramble to her knees and wind her arms around his neck.

"I'm sorry," she said, weeping afresh. "I'm so sorry for your—disappointment. It is so lonely with no one to love."

It was so long since anyone had asked anything of him but his professional skill that he had forgotten the felicity of being needed, and as he held her, weeping against his breast, the

unfamiliar thought struck him that perhaps he still had something left to give. He remembered Miranda once saying to him,
"Children need affection, Adam, or they get sick."

"Don't feel lonely, my dear," he said, his fingers gently
exploring the hollow at the nape of her neck. "I'm not very
good at handling my household, I'm afraid, but I'll always listen
and try to understand. Now, we must start being sensible. I want
to take that temperature and get you off to bed."

THE STORM had broken as Adam finally shook down the thermometer and returned it to its case.

"Nervous of storms?" he had asked. "It's over Ram's Tor
way, I think, and will probably pass us by." She shook her head
and he observed her with a critical eye. "You've got a pretty
high fever, young woman. If you're not better in the morning
I'll get Tregellis to come in and have a look at you."

"I do not want Dr. Tregellis," she said tearfully.

"Why not?"

"He doesn't like me."

He looked surprised but only said evasively, "Well, we'll
see."

He examined her carefully, then sent her up to bed where he
firmly kept her for several days. At first she had not been
conscious of very much except the ache in her bones and the
shivering fits that curiously made her hot instead of cold. She
was aware of Adam in and out of the room and of the firmness
and coolness of his hands, and she remembered him saying, just
before she dropped off to sleep, "I'm leaving the door open. If
you want anything in the night you have only to call. I shall
probably come and have a look at you, anyway."

What door, she thought, confused. But much later on she woke
to find him standing by her bed in his dressing gown. There was
a light in his room and the door between was open.

"Oh, *that* door," she said, and smiled at him sleepily.
"What is the time?"

"Nearly half-past three. Are the aches any better? Good.

Well, we'll just see what your temperature is doing now, then you can go back to sleep.''

After that first night it was only, Adam said, a matter of rest and care. A bad chill combined with mental shock could produce symptoms quite as alarming as something more serious.

Simmy brought Fay to see her one afternoon. The child stood just inside the doorway, staring at her with big eyes.

''Come and sit on the bed, my rabbit,'' Miranda invited, but Fay only advanced to the middle of the room and continued to stand there silently.

''It is usual to ask after the invalid's health,'' Miranda said, smiling at her.

Miss Simms turned to Fay and said, in her colorless voice, ''I think you have an apology to make to Mrs. Chantry. Don't you remember what I told you to say?''

''I'm sorry I made you ill and I'm sorry for the poor little bird,'' Fay said glibly.

Miranda looked at the governess.

''Simmy, do you mind?'' she asked gently. ''I think Fay will have more to say for herself if you leave us.''

For a moment Miss Simms made no move to go, and Miranda thought she was preparing one of her quiet refusals to relinquish authority.

''Mr. Chantry gave orders that I was not to allow you to be upset in any way,'' Miss Simms said then.

''Did he? Well, I see no reason why Fay should upset me.'' Miranda was smiling but firm. ''Do not worry, Simmy. I will send her back to you in a little while.''

''Very well, Mrs. Chantry.'' Simmy's long, sallow face was closed and shuttered again, but before she left the room she gave the silent child a warning glance. ''Remember what I told you Fay. Your father will be sure to ask how you behaved when he comes home.''

''What *did* she tell you?'' Miranda asked idly, when they were alone.

''She said Adam would send me away to something called a

reform school if I upset you," Fay said sullenly. "A place where they only have wicked children—like the prison at Princetown."

Something cold touched Miranda. She remembered that the child invented stories to the point of lying, but there was a ring of truth in this statement that was disturbing. Before she could reply, Fay cried suddenly, "Did I really make you ill, Miranda? Would I have been responsible if you d-died?"

"No, of course not," Miranda said swiftly. "I got a chill. I was never going to die, my silly cabbage."

The child's face crumpled as the tears came, and Miranda held out her arms.

"Come," she said softly, and Fay ran to her and flung herself weeping across the bed. Miranda held her closely and for the first time she felt that Fay was just a normal little girl beset by the exaggerated fears of childhood and seeking reassurance in a child's natural way. This was not the usual scene to attract attention. The child was genuinely upset, and when her tears subsided into sniffs she looked at Miranda with shy contrition.

"Now," Miranda said, wiping the wet lashes with a corner of the sheet, "you will tell me truthfully—did Simmy really say that your father would send you away to this place you spoke of?"

"Oh, yes," said Fay.

"But Adam never told you so, did he?"

"N-no." Fay sounded doubtful. "But he must have told Simmy, mustn't he?"

"No, my little one, never would he suggest such a thing. Reform schools are for criminals, not for little girls who are naughty and sometimes tell lies. Your father would not even let you go to a nice school, where children make friends with other children, for fear you would not be happy."

"Simmy said I was wicked to kill the bird."

"Not wicked, Fay—unkind, though I do not think you meant to be."

"No, no, I didn't." The child's eyes were afraid. "I didn't mean to be unkind to the kitten, either, but Simmy said I was."

"The kitten?"

"The kitten Nanny sent me once. Simmy took it away."
Miranda remembered now.

"What had you done to the kitten?" she asked gently.

"Nothing. I loved it. I called it Nanny because she gave it to
me and one day I dressed it in my baby doll's bonnet and long
clothes and Simmy said I was cruel. She sent it away before
Adam could come home and punish me."

"I see," said Miranda slowly, and at the same moment there
was a knock on the door. Without waiting for a reply, the
governess slipped quietly into the room.

"I said I would send Fay back to you in a little while,
Simmy," Miranda said a little sharply.

Miss Simms looked at them, her pale eyes observing Miranda's heightened color, the child's tear-stained face, and the
huddled little picture they presented in the disarranged bed.

"I think it's time I took this little girl away," she said
smoothly. "You look very flushed, Mrs. Chantry. Has Fay
been making up fairy tales for you?"

"Fairy tales are not true," said Miranda, giving her a level
look.

Simmy replied in her expressionless voice, "Exactly, but we
both know what little people are, don't we? You should be
resting, Mrs. Chantry. Come along, Fay."

The child slipped off the bed without a word, but she turned
and gave Miranda one quick kiss before joining the governess.
For a moment they stood there together, and Miranda looked at
Simmy. She was like the house, Miranda thought uneasily. Her
face had the same secret, shuttered look of Wintersbride on that
gray, misty evening in May, and she remembered that once
before she had thought that, like the house, Simmy did not
always reveal her true personality.

"Come and see me tomorrow, *chérie*," she said, ignoring the
governess. "We will plan a little treat for when I am well."

Fay did not answer, and Miss Simms, smiling politely,
shepherded her out of the room.

When Adam came to see Miranda that evening, he frowned as

he laid a hand on her forehead and observed the brightness of her eyes.

"You're overexcited," he said. "I shall have to tell Simmy to keep Fay away until you're fit again."

"No, no," she said quickly, catching his hand. "I wish to speak to you about that, Adam. I think it is Simmy who makes trouble between you and Fay. She tells or implies things that are not true."

"Nonsense," he said, and sat down on the side of the bed. "Simmy has already spoken to me. She gathered that Fay had been upsetting you."

Miranda gave an angry bounce in the bed.

"Fay did not upset me," she said. "But Simmy has been putting ideas into her head. She makes you out to be a monster—a bogeyman. Do you know that she told the child you would send her to a reform school? Is it any wonder that she cannot love you?"

"Miranda, my dear," he said a little wearily. "You should know by now that Fay invents things. I know very well Simmy never said anything of the sort. Is it likely, now?"

"Fay was not inventing, this time," Miranda said stubbornly. "She was just a normal little girl frightened by bogies. And, Adam, that story about the kitten—I do not know what Simmy told you, but it was not true. All children dress their pets up in dolls' clothes—that is not cruel."

"Is that what Fay told you?"

"Yes, and I believe it. You were not there, so how do you know what was the truth?"

"My dear child, what reason would Simmy have for lying?"

"I don't know. But I do know she is keeping Fay from you. She uses you as a threat—a bogeyman, as I told you. She would not even leave us alone together this afternoon because she was afraid I might learn something."

His fingers went automatically to her pulse.

"This won't do," he told her severely. "If you're going to react like this to Fay's visits then I must forbid her this room until you're well again."

"No," she said.

He looked at her flushed face and began to speak reasonably and patiently as if she was a stubborn child.

"Miranda, dear, believe me, this isn't the first time Fay has invented stories for gullible listeners. She's tried it on Grace, who was too sensible to pay much attention. You are young and more easily swayed, but Simmy hasn't been with me all these years for nothing. I rely on her implicitly and if it hadn't been for her my poor little daughter would have been more of a problem than she is. Now, I'm going to give you something to make you sleep, and in the morning you'll see things in their right proportions again."

THE DAYS DRIFTED BY LAZILY, and Miranda enjoyed her rest in bed, for here she was safe from Wintersbride and that other secret life the house would not reveal.

"I've been thinking," Adam said the evening before she was to get up for the first time, "would you like me to take you away somewhere for a bit?"

She looked surprised.

"Mr. Benyon has been talking to you?" she asked.

"He thinks we both need a holiday. How does the idea appeal to you? We might try the south of France."

"Of course, if you would like," she said politely.

He observed her thoughtfully. He respected her uncharacteristically guarded reticence, for had not he himself dealt in the same commodity for years? It was his own fault if she adhered so literally to the terms of their marriage, and he was beginning to suspect that only a fool would have imagined that such an arrangement was feasible—a fool such as himself, and a very young girl like Miranda persuading herself and him that she was not romantic.

"What are you smiling at?" she asked him.

"You. You are rather absurd, aren't you?"

"I do not think so," she replied with dignity. "I cannot help it that I am not very tall and wearing no shoes and—"

"No, but that isn't quite what I meant. However—shall we

have our holiday, or shall I do as I had originally intended and run up to Scotland by myself when I can spare the time?''

"I would like very much to come away with you," she said a little shyly, and wondered whether, should they both be free of Wintersbride and all it signified for a while, he might, perhaps, find a natural need for her. "When could we go?"

"It depends how I'm fixed," he said vaguely. "In the meantime you must build yourself up and not take too much out of yourself."

She looked at him sitting in the circle of lamplight by her bed—at his graying hair, the strong lines of self-discipline, and the dark eyes that could dwell on her with an interest that was coldly professional but could also be tender—and it seemed a long time since he, a stranger, had brought her to his home with such little thought as to the consequences.

"Why did you marry me?" she asked, and he raised his eyebrows.

"Is this your famous habit of speaking your thoughts aloud or is it a serious question?" he asked.

She looked at him under her lashes.

"A little of both, I suppose. I think what I really meant was why did you choose me when you did not know anything about me and only thought of me as a child?"

He considered, wondering a little himself. He supposed that the piquancy of that first meeting must have unconsciously influenced him. At the time she had seemed a child, a little waif who could not be abandoned to a world in which she had no place. But was this, along with the fact that he himself needed a wife, the only reason he had married her?

"It's hard to say now, Miranda," he replied slowly. "An impulse, shall we say? A way out of both our difficulties? But now I think you should settle down for the night. In a day or two, when I see how much I'm committed to in my professional engagements, we'll make plans for going away. Good night."

He stood for a moment, looking down at her, then unexpectedly stooped and kissed her on the forehead.

BUT THE PLANS were never made. Adam was apologetic but said it was impossible for him to get away that month or even the next. Miranda was disappointed but unsurprised. She had not really expected that he would take her away. The next morning, however, there was a package on her breakfast tray and Nancy was greatly impressed by the large cut-glass bottle of perfume that Miranda unwrapped.

"Oh, my!" she exclaimed, touching it with reverence. "'Tis a proper job and no mistake. Is it from the master, ma'am?"

"Yes," Miranda said, fingering Adam's card.

Nancy went back to the servants' hall, warm with approval. That was more like it, she told Bessie, thinking of those pillows on the other half of the big bed whose spotless covers she changed each week because Mrs. Yeo would have been after her if she hadn't. She liked Miranda, who treated her as an equal and did not put on airs.

Miranda let her breakfast get cold as she admired her present. No one had ever given her perfume before, and it was a luxury she had not been able to afford for herself prior to her marriage. And although Adam was now giving her a generous allowance, it had never occurred to her to be so extravagant.

She picked up the card again. On the back of it he had written in evident haste, "For a charming young lady, whom I hate to disappoint."

Had he minded the postponement of his plans after all? Did he perhaps lack sufficient encouragement to break down such reserves as he might feel in view of their mutual bargain?

"How," she demanded aloud, "does one encourage a man whose only interest in bodies is how to carve them up!" And she began recklessly to splash perfume all over her person: behind her ears, in the thin hollow of her throat, in the curve of her elbows and between her slight breasts.

"There!" she said, flinging herself back in the bed and stretching luxuriously. "Now I smell like a *demimondaine*."

When Adam came home that evening she ran across the hall to meet him and stood on tiptoe, offering him the top of her head to smell.

"Am I not a fine lady now?" she laughed. "See, I have it behind the ears, on the crown of the head and—oh, everywhere possible. Can you smell it, Adam?"

"I should think they could smell it in the servant's hall," he observed, liking the feel of her soft curls under his chin.

"There is too much?" she asked anxiously. "It has, perhaps, gone to my head a little. You see, I have never had perfume before."

"It has certainly gone to your head in more senses than one," he replied, but his voice was indulgent and he unexpectedly dropped a light kiss on the top of her curls "I'm glad you're pleased, Miranda. I'm rather a neglectful husband, I'm afraid."

"Oh, no," she protested, shocked. "You have given me a ring, a string of pearls, a new toilet set, and *all* my expensive clothes. How can you say you are neglectful?"

He touched her eager face with tender fingers.

"You are a very delightful recipient. I must do it more often," he said gently, and thought of Melisande, who had taken gifts for granted and assessed them only for their worth.

To Miranda it was an evening different from any other. Adam for once had forgotten his work, or perhaps he was making a special effort to please her. He was, she knew, atoning gracefully for the promise he could not fulfil, and she was content to forget the hints of Simmy and Arthur Benyon in the pleasure of such unusual intimacy.

How charming he could be when he took the trouble, she thought, her eyes watching him lovingly across the dinner table; how attractive his hair was, shining like frost in the candlelight.

"Did you go gray very young?" she inquired, desiring to know all the small, unimportant things he never told her about himself.

"Pretty young," he replied with a smile. "It runs in my family. Do my gray hairs dismay you, Miranda?"

"Oh, no," she said. "It is very becoming, and also most distinguished in your profession. Tell me of when you were a boy, Adam. Where did you live? Had you brothers or sisters?"

He glanced across at her a little wryly. Married for two

months and she had still to ask him for the simple information of first acquaintance! He told her a little about his boyhood in Cumberland. His father had been a doctor, practicing until the day he died because he loved medicine, although there had been no need for such selfless hard work since he had married a rich woman. There were no other children, and later, when Adam had finished his training and wished to specialize, his mother's death had made it both possible and easy to build a reputation without the customary pinching and slogging.

"I was one of the lucky ones," he told Miranda with a rather bitter little smile. "By the time I was twenty-eight I was well on my way to being established in my profession and had a wife and a child and a rosy future predicted by the high-ups. It just goes to show that you should never tempt providence."

"How did you tempt providence?" she asked, a little afraid, for some reason, of the answer.

But he only replied, with the bitterness still touching the corners of his mouth, "If I hadn't had a considerable private income I could never have afforded to marry at twenty-six and things might have been very different. But that applies to anything, doesn't it?"

She had come to like the little paneled room where they usually sat after dinner, but in the brighter glow of electricity, the atmosphere seemed subtly to change. Adam was already looking at his watch and saying he had work to do, and she knew that very soon he would retire to his study and she would not see him again.

She slipped a hand through his arm.

"Not tonight," she pleaded. "You are tired. Stay here with me until bedtime, or walk with me in the garden."

He looked down at her, surprised and a little touched. It was the first time she had ever tried to detain him.

"I'm afraid you must find the evenings dull," he said.

"No, no, the others I do not mind, but tonight is different. *You* are different."

"Am I? And you, I'm beginning to suspect, are a bit of a minx."

"A minx? Oh, no. A minx can always get what she wants. How can I keep you, Adam? By flattery, by tears? But you would not like tears and I would not dare to flatter. Will you sniff me again, please? I think the perfume must be wearing off."

She had offered him the top of her curls again and he regarded her with an odd expression.

"Is it possible you are trying to flirt with me, Miranda?" he asked.

She looked up at him.

"Yes," she replied with firmness.

His eyebrows lifted, a trifle sardonically.

"That might be rather dangerous in the circumstances," he said softly. "I'm flesh and blood, you know, in spite of our platonic agreement."

"Our agreement was of your making," she said, the heavy lashes veiling her eyes.

"Yours, too, remember. We struck a bargain, Miranda, but if you try me too hard, one of these days you'll have to take the consequences and how would you like that?"

She slid her hands to his shoulders, but she would not meet his eyes.

"I cannot know beforehand, can I?" she said.

He put a hand under her chin, forcing her to look at him, and she saw that although the quizzical smile remained, his eyes were grave and suddenly demanding.

"If I thought—" he began, then the telephone started to ring insistently in his study.

"Damn!" he exclaimed, and went out of the room to answer it.

Miranda waited, her hands pressed to cheeks that were suddenly hot. *He will think me shameless,* she thought, then remembered the look in his eyes and was afraid and glad at the same time.

The moment he returned she knew that her evening was over.

"That was an emergency call from the hospital," he told her.

"I haven't time to change. Be a good girl and phone Bidder while I collect my things."

She was conscious of him moving about the room as she made the call. Drawers opened and shut, his case snapped to, and he was ready. She went with him into the hall. For a moment he became aware of her, of how silent and small she was as she listened for the car.

He ruffled her fair hair.

"Saved by the telephone!" he said with a little quirk of humor. "You might have had a narrow escape, my child. Don't do it again."

He was gone before she could make any reply.

CHAPTER NINE

MIRANDA AWOKE the next morning with a sense of loss. The evening had been so exceptional, so sweet to think back on, and the telephone cutting in upon that strange new intimacy had left her without courage for the future. Could a mood, so fragile, be recaptured? Had she the courage to offer again what might not be wanted? She remembered Arthur Benyon's words: "Your husband is a very lonely man."

Adam . . . . She remembered how he had smiled and called her a strange child when she had quoted the Bible upon learning his Christian name, and she remembered again her own voice saying, "And the Lord God said, It is not good that the man should be alone; I will make him a helpmeet for him. . . ."

Miranda stretched her slender arms above her head. God had made her, she thought soberly, not, perhaps in the same likeness that He had created Melisande, but fair enough to suffice a man's needs. Was it not Eve who had offered the apple to Adam? Was it not, as Pierre had once said, the woman who should command the situation?

The morning passed pleasantly in solitary idleness, and Miranda selected, with great care, a posy for Adam's room. She lingered lovingly over each bloom, arranging and rearranging them in the *famille verte* bowl she had stolen from the drawing room, then she carried the bowl upstairs and into Adam's bedroom.

Miranda put her bowl of flowers on the dressing table and there she saw, tucked into a corner of the frame of the mirror, a small snapshot, the only incongruous detail in the well-ordered room. It was a snapshot of herself, and Miranda stared at it, touched by the curling edges and absurdly grateful for that unexpected evidence of sentiment in Adam. She touched the photograph with gentle fingers, set it more firmly in its place and went softly from the room.

She was at the head of the stairs when she heard the telephone ring. It was quicker to go back to Adam's bedroom where there was an extension, than to his study, but even so she was too late.

"I think she must be out," Simmy's quiet voice was saying, and Miranda thought there was a hint of disappointment in Adam's reply.

"Oh, very well, don't bother. Just tell her I'm sorry but I can't get home tonight. I'll call again in the morning."

"Adam, wait—I'm here," Miranda said, but he had hung up and she heard the soft click of the receiver being put down in the study.

Disappointment, sharp and irrational, drove the tears to her eyes and she ran down the stairs. Simmy was just coming out of Adam's study and before she could speak, Miranda cried angrily, "Why did you say I was out? You saw me going upstairs with that bowl of flowers not twenty minutes ago."

Miss Simms looked at her, her pale eyes expressionless.

"I don't recollect seeing you, Mrs. Chantry," she replied. "In any case it was not important. Mr. Chantry was only calling to say he would not be home tonight."

"That is not the point," said Miranda, remembering how many times Simmy had taken messages and not troubled to fetch her to the telephone. "I wished to speak to my husband as it happens, and you knew very well I was only upstairs."

A faint smile touched the governess's thin lips.

"My dear Mrs. Chantry, why should I wish to prevent you from speaking to your husband?"

"I do not know," Miranda answered uncertainly. "But it happens too often. In future will you be so kind as to take the trouble to look for me first?"

Almost for the first time since she had known her, Miranda saw the faint color mount under the tired skin.

"I'm not a servant, Mrs. Chantry," Simmy said. "The late

Mrs. Chantry would never have dreamed of speaking to me like that.''

"I daresay not. But you,'' observed Miranda with sudden shrewdness, ''would never have dreamed of treating her like an inconsequent child.''

A strange expression crossed the governess's face.

"An inconsequent child . . .'' she said slowly, almost as if she was talking to herself. ''Yes . . . that's what she became . . . a child who relied on one person. . . .'' She raised her eyes and looked straight at Miranda. ''No, Mrs. Chantry, it was not her husband she relied on, it was me,'' she said with an odd little ring of triumph, and went quickly up the stairs.

Miranda stood quite still, looking after her. There was a chill in the house, and watching the thin, drab figure of the governess turning the bend in the stairs without a backward glance, Miranda had the strange impression that Simmy *was* Wintersbride, cold, secret and hostile, and the child in her barred schoolroom and even she herself were prisoners.

"Simmy!'' she called running to the foot of the stairs. ''I would like to take Fay for a picnic lunch—just the two of us. Will you tell her to get ready?''

For a moment she thought Miss Simms was going to refuse outright, but she only said, ''Very well, Mrs. Chantry,'' in a tight, repressed voice and went on up the stairs.

It was a pleasant picnic, and for the first time Miranda saw Fay as a different child from the difficult, self-centered young creature who had to be treated so carefully. Away from the house and the governess she was just a normal little girl delighted with an unexpected treat. She splashed happily in the river and played games of Miranda's invention with the shy curiosity of a child who has lacked companionship too long.

"Would you like to go to school?'' Miranda asked idly, as exhausted and content they lay on their backs in the cool bracken.

"Yes,'' said Fay unexpectedly. ''But Simmy says Adam would never allow it. I used to be given books about girls who had midnight feasts and saved the honor of the school. They were exciting.'' It sounded odd coming from a child who hid novelettes under her pillow and talked so often like a sophisticated adult. "Simmy says those books aren't true. She doesn't allow me to read them anymore.''

"They are as true as the stories Nancy brings you,'' Miranda said. "We will go to Plymouth together and buy some more, yes?''

"It wouldn't do any good,'' Fay replied, tickling Miranda's nose with a piece of grass. "Besides, I don't think I would like school, really. Bidder drove us to Princeton once for a picnic and Simmy showed me the prison and said school would be just like that.''

"Simmy told you that?'' exclaimed Miranda sharply. "But, Fay, that is not true. You should ask your father about these things.''

"Adam doesn't like me,'' the child said, but she spoke with less conviction than usual. "Simmy says he can't help it. I remind him too much of my mother.''

Had the governess, thought Miranda indignantly, deliberately set out to turn the child against her father? It was beginning to look to her very much as if Adam was being used as the familiar bogeyman of tradition.

"Listen, my rabbit,'' she said. "It is true you are like your mother, but it is not true that your father dislikes you. It is he, Fay, who thinks you dislike him. You have not, I think, been very kind to him.''

"You can't,'' said Fay with innocent conviction, "be unkind to grown-ups.''

"You can be unkind to anyone, *chérie*—often without knowing it,'' Miranda said. "You were unkind to me When I first came here and wanted to make friends with you.''

"You aren't exactly a grown-up,'' Fay said slowly, "but I didn't know, then. Simmy had said that Adam had put you in my mother's place and would love you better than me.''

"But,'' said Miranda gently, "if you do not want your father's love, why should you mind?''

The child looked puzzled.

"I don't know," she said on a note of surprise. "I only know what Simmy tells me."

"That," said Miranda with a certain grimness, "becomes very evident. Listen, my cabbage, do not believe all the good Simmy tells you."

"You mean she tells lies?"

"No, no—but she, perhaps, misunderstands. When you are puzzled, ask me. I will always explain the truth."

"Yes, Miranda. I'm sorry I was unkind to you. I love you very much now, though Simmy says I only think I do."

Miranda gave the child a quick kiss and was touched to feel the eager response from the warm young lips.

"As long as you think you do, that is what matters," she said. "Now, we will find some flowers and then we must go home for tea. I will be in trouble, you know, for I have kept you from your afternoon rest."

"Why does Simmy not allow you to go to Shap Tor?" Miranda asked curiously as they paused to watch a herd of ponies gallop over the shoulder of the hill.

"I don't know," Fay replied. "Once, Nancy took me, and Simmy was very angry. It's a lovely place for hide-and-seek, too. The quarry echoes."

"We will go by ourselves one day and play hide-and-seek together," said Miranda.

But the day ended badly. They were very late for tea, and Simmy met them, white and angry, and ordered the child to bed as soon as she had had her tea.

"But why do you punish her?" Miranda asked indignantly. "She has not done wrong."

"It is a precaution, not a punishment," Miss Simms said. "She has missed her rest and got overexcited and we shall probably have a scene. Fay, don't hang around Mrs. Chantry's neck in that silly fashion. She doesn't like it."

When, later, Miranda went upstairs to Fay's room she was met by Simmy, who said she did not wish the child to be disturbed.

"I have had a difficult time with her," she said, her back to the closed door. "She has settled down now and I think it unwise to disturb her again."

Miranda looked at her steadily.

"Very well," she said, "but do not try to set Fay against me, Simmy. She is a naturally affectionate child, and you, I think, do not like that."

A flicker of the old malice showed for an instant in the governess's eyes, but she only said, "I should not dream of trying to set the child against you, but you must remember I've witnessed these little—crushes—before. You are the one who will get hurt, Mrs. Chantry, not Fay."

"As her father was hurt?" asked Miranda gently.

The sallow face seemed to grow longer.

"The position there is unfortunate, I admit, but understandable in the circumstances. The child is heartbreakingly like her mother. Every time he looks at her—but, forgive me, I should not be saying that to you. Mr. Chantry must surely have got over his first wife's death since he has married again."

There was a hint of mockery in her colorless voice, and Miranda found herself flushing.

"We were not discussing my husband's feelings about marriage," she said. "I was trying to say that I find Fay is very suggestible, and I think you have not always been—wise—in your care of her."

A slight smile touched Simmy's lips, as if she recognized an adversary and did not deny her own intentions.

"You are very young, Mrs. Chantry, and only lately come among us," she replied. "But may I say that it's not altogether wise to put foolish ideas into the child's head. As you say yourself, she is very suggestible. Good night."

ADAM TELEPHONED AFTER BREAKFAST and she thought there was a different note in his voice.

"I was so sorry I was kept last night," he said, and she knew that for him, too, the interruption had been a disappointment. "I'll be home early to make up. What would you like me to bring you for a present?"

"A pumpkin," she said, laughing softly. "A pumpkin and six white mice to carry us away from Wintersbride."

"Do you want to be carried away from Wintersbride?" he asked, lingering with unusual tolerance over the absurd conversation.

"No," she said. "Not so long as you are there. I am determined now to become a minx and get what I want."

"Are you?" There was a little pause. "Well, I gave you fair warning the other night. You must make yourself responsible for the consequences of any ill-considered action on your part."

He was laughing at her, but she thought he was warning her, too.

"Yes, Adam. I told you I have the practical point of view," she said demurely, and giggled suddenly. "Simmy says I must remember you are far too busy to waste time with unimportant chatter. Are you in the middle of a consultation?"

"Hardly! Well, I suppose we'd better take Simmy's advice and hang up. Miranda—"

"Yes?"

"Shall we—make it a celebration tonight?"

She cupped her hands lovingly around the receiver and her voice was suddenly serious and a little shy.

"Yes . . ." she said.

"Then wear your prettiest dress. Goodbye, darling," he said, and hang up.

Miranda stood with the receiver still in her hands. *Darling* . . . he had never called her that before. . . . How strange that it should immediately bring him so close.

Before she put the receiver back she thought she heard the faint click of the extension being returned to its rest. Had someone been listening in?

It was a happy day of growing anticipation for Miranda. "Make it a celebration," he had said, so she spent the hours arranging the tiny details that, to her, should mark a special occasion: lavish flower decorations for the table, the Sèvres dinner service, the Waterford glass, and a carefully chosen menu with the appropriate wines.

"Were you expecting company, madam?" Mrs. Yeo inquired, eyeing the preparations in the dining room with surprise.

"Only my husband," said Miranda shyly, and unexpectedly and astonishingly, Mrs. Yeo smiled.

"Well, I must say that's nice to hear when a lady takes trouble over her gentleman," she said, and looked at Miranda with the first hint of approval she had ever allowed herself.

"Mrs. Yeo—" encouraged by the woman's unusual friendliness, Miranda grew bold "—I am a very good cook, you know. Would you mind very much if this afternoon I prepared some little French dishes? I could, of course, do so if I wish, but I would like your permission first, and I will not, I promise you, make disorder in your kitchen."

She waited breathlessly for Mrs. Yeo's shocked refusal, but the housekeeper regarded her with a certain surprised indulgence and said mildly, "Well, I take it very kindly that you should ask me, madam—very handsome indeed—not like some I could mention, in and out of my kitchen with never a by-your-leave and taking this and that for the schoolroom without asking if it can be spared. I've no objection to you trying your hand at a little cooking now and then."

"Thank you, Mrs. Yeo," said Miranda, feeling rather bewildered.

Had Simmy and Mrs. Yeo had words that the housekeeper was suddenly so obliging? For the first time it occurred to her that the rest of his staff might not share Adam's own belief in the governess's integrity, and she warmed toward the hitherto obstructive Mrs. Yeo.

Miranda had never enjoyed an afternoon at Wintersbride so much. Unlike the rest of the house, the big kitchen was bright and friendly. Selecting her ingredients and cooking utensils with the precision of a general planning a maneuver, she was reminded of the old days when she had cooked for her father and Pierre and been awarded unfailing praise.

Fay, having been informed privately of what was going on, came down to help and thrust inquisitive fingers into bowls and saucepans. Miranda tied aprons around both of them and the kitchen rang with their laughter while the summer rain beat against the windows, a pleasant and fitting accompaniment to an occupation that kept them all indoors.

They had all forgotten Simmy, and when she appeared in the kitchen at teatime, having searched the house in vain, Miranda felt bound to ask her to join them.

Miss Simms stood surveying the prepared dishes with eyebrows that slowly rose.

"Dear me!" she remarked. "It all looks very lavish and extravagant. Is this a special occasion, might I ask?"

"Yes," said Miranda, wiping a streak of flour from her flushed face, too excited to remember the unpleasantness of yesterday. "It is a special occasion for me. A celebration."

"Oh? Well, I hope your efforts won't be wasted," the governess replied, and Miranda was sure then that Simmy had been listening on the extension that morning. "Come along, Fay, dear. You may eat your scones in the schoolroom."

"But, Simmy, we are having tea *here*," said Fay. "Kitchen tea, Miranda said, with Nancy and the girl, and Bessie is to have a tray in the servants' hall because she's too grand."

"That in itself is a very foolish idea to put into a little girl's head," Miss Simms said to no one in particular. "You've had enough excitement for one afternoon, dear. Remember how yesterday ended. You don't want me to ask your father to keep you altogether in the schoolroom if you can't behave, do you?"

Miranda supposed the ensuing storm of tears was inevitable, and she wondered a little curiously how Simmy enjoyed being a perpetual cause of grief in the little girl. Then her eyes widened as she observed the governess's face and realized that she did enjoy it.

Simmy, as was her wont on such occasions, waited impassively for the storm to subside, and in the middle of it all Miranda rushed too late to the oven and discovered that Fay's scones were burned black.

"*Ah, chérie, quelle domage!*" Miranda exclaimed, French coming quickest to her tongue in the face of catastrophe. "You cannot let your attention be distracted when you are cooking, or suffer the interruptions. Never mind, my rabbit, we will make some more another time, and next time you will watch them and we will not allow the interruptions.''

''Well, Mrs. Chantry,'' said Miss Simms in a curious voice. ''You certainly have a strange way of upholding authority. I'm afraid I shall have to speak to Fay's father about certain little matters, after all—in fact, as soon as he returns.''

Miranda looked at her. ''If you,'' she said very quietly, heedless of the presence of Nancy and the girl, ''upset my husband unnecessarily, Simmy, I shall have no hesitation in warning him that you listen to his conversations on the telephone.''

For a moment, Simmy's pale lashes flickered with some sign of emotion. Then she said in a colorless voice, ''What a very extraordinary suggestion to make in front of the servants, Mrs. Chantry. Come along, Fay. We won't wait for the tea tray under the circumstances. Nancy can bring it up when it's ready.''

''Well, beggar me!'' exclaimed Nancy as soon as the door had closed, forgetting, in the excitement of the moment, that she was not at home with her free-spoken family. ''Do she really listen in, ma'am?''

''Yes,'' said Miranda angrily, ''I'm sure she does.''

''Oh, my dear soul! Fancy you'm telling her in front of me and the girl. Her'll not forget that.''

''No, I suppose not, but it's time Miss Simms understood that all in this house are not fooled by her little ways.''

Miranda had ceased to think of Nancy as the maid who brought her breakfast up each morning. They were just two young girls united in a common cause.

''Has it ever struck you, Nancy, that Fay is only silly and difficult when Miss Simms is around?'' she asked, beginning to untie her apron.

Nancy considered, her head to one side.

''Now I come to think on it, you'm right,'' she said. ''Though Miss Simms always says it's others that upsets Miss Fay and her's the one that has to suffer for it afterward. I don't know, I'm sure. Since you'm come her's a nicer little girl, I will allow, but Miss Simms don't like her away from the schoolroom for long."

"Are Mrs. Yeo and Miss Simms not good friends, then?"

"Well, I wouldn't say that, but they was both here in the late mistress's time, you see, and I reckon they both think they have their rights. There's always been a bit of feeling between the schoolroom and the servants' hall."

"Yes, I suppose there would be. What happened to Nanny?"

"Nanny?" Nancy laughed. "Oh, her's long before my time. Left under a cloud, I did hear, but no one seems to rightly know—it was a brave little while ago."

"But Mrs. Yeo would know, wouldn't she?"

"Yes, I suppose. But her's not one to chitter." Nancy suddenly remembered the girl, silent and openmouthed with a fine tale to take back to the village that evening.

"You start clearing up this litter," she said sharply. "And don't 'ee get scranny ideas because the mistress chooses to be a bit free with her tongue."

She grinned apologetically at Miranda, and started to get the schoolroom tray ready.

MIRANDA DID NOT STOP for tea in the kitchen after all. She wanted to recapture the delights of anticipation that Simmy had so nearly destroyed, and she wanted to make sure that she was the first to greet Adam on his return and so postpone, if she could not evade, the governess's small threat to her happiness.

She had her bath early and spent a long time selecting a dress. In the end she chose the simple gray chiffon with the cherry sash because she had worn it on her wedding night. She slipped on her ring, clasped the pearls about her neck and finally touched her skin with perfume, careful not to overdo it this time.

"I am decked with his gifts," she said aloud, her eyes suddenly grave. "And I—what gifts have I?"

The answer was still unclear, but her mouth was touched with a shy ardency and to this, at least, she knew the answer.

I must be bold, she thought, *but not demanding. . . . I must be wise and inviting . . . and I must have the courage to persuade him should he still think of her. . . . For if it is true, as I told him, that it is not difficult to love any man who is decent, can that not be true for him, also . . .?*

She gave herself a little shake and ran downstairs to the dining room to put the last touches to the table.

Although it was not yet seven o'clock, the evening was dark. A small wood fire had been lighted in the study because, Miranda had thought, *firelight is romantic, and when we leave the candles in the dining room we will not turn on the lights.*

She did not hear the car, but a soft tap on the window pane made her jump, and she turned, a little startled, to look over her shoulder. A man's figure stood outlined against the early twilight, and she ran to unlatch the French windows and let him in. She flung open the doors, then stood staring incredulously at the man who stepped inside.

"But—but it *cannot* be!" she stammered, as if she had herself conjured up a dream from the shadows and firelight.

"But yes, it is I, *chérie*, and I will say first of all that it is of the inconvenience most unnecessary that you live in the middle of a moor," he said, and now she knew he was really Pierre, complaining of inconveniences as if she had seen him only yesterday.

"Pierre . . . Pierre . . ." she cried, half laughing, half crying . "I cannot *believe* . . . oh, you are so wet!"

She shut the windows while he took off his raincoat, flinging it with his old carelessness in a heap on the floor. Then he switched on the lights.

"Now," he said, surveying her critically, "let me look at my little Mielle who has grown up and found herself a husband without consulting her old friend. *Très charmante, ma petite* . . . a fine gown . . . jewels . . . a big house . . . but you have not changed, I think."

"And you," she said, watching him with eyes hungry for a renewal of her happy childhood, "you have not changed either. Oh, *Pierre* . . . ."

She ran to him and threw her arms around his neck.

"It has been so long," she said. "And I thought you had forgotten me. Pierre—where is Marguerite?"

"Marguerite? Still in the château with her family."

"Then you did not marry her after all?"

"No, her parents would not permit. They married her off to the Comte de Vilbois and they all live *en famille* at the château."

"That funny little man with the tic? Oh, poor Marguerite—she thought you were such a *beau garçon*."

He held her away from him for a moment.

"But you, my rabbit, you did not wait," he said, and her eyes widened.

"For you? But, Pierre, it was you who always counseled me to be practical."

"Yes, yes, I talked too much. But now, we meet for a little moment, yes, and things are as they were."

Even as she kissed him, she knew that for her, things could never be as they were. Circumstances, life itself, had changed since those carefree days in France, and while she welcomed Pierre's return with the innocent gladness of her childhood, he was no longer the loved one, the only friend.

"You smell as you never did in those other days," he was saying, with laughter in his voice as he rubbed his cheek against hers.

"The perfume you cared about was fish and paint," she said and, pulling out of his arms, saw Adam standing in the doorway.

She was still too lost in old memories to be warned by the expression on his face as he stood there, watching them. She only knew that here was the perfect reunion, her husband and her childhood friend, and she stretched out a hand to him.

"Adam, is it not wonderful?" she said. "This is Pierre, of whom I have so often told you. And you see, he had not forgotten me as I feared, and he did not even marry Marguerite. Pierre—this is my husband."

The young man looked with frank curiosity at the man Miranda had married, and although Pierre came forward at once with graceful apologies, Adam had seen the look of surprise in his eyes.

"You will forgive me, *m'sieur*, for arriving so unexpectedly, but I sail from Plymouth tomorrow and I had a wish to see my little friend again," he said, and bowed politely.

"I haven't the pleasure of knowing your name, but how do you do?" said Adam in an expressionless voice.

"Morel," Pierre said, bowing again. "Pierre Morel."

"But you will, naturally, call him Pierre," broke in Miranda. "And he will stay the night, of course, will he not, Adam?"

"Of course," said Adam, after a slight pause. "Now if you will both excuse me, I will go and change."

Pierre made a small grimace.

"He is not pleased, the good husband," he said, and Miranda, released from the old spell, faced reality with a sense of dismay. That it should be this of all times that Pierre should choose to visit her—that on such an evening the incalculable should happen!

"It is better that I should go back to Plymouth, *hein*?" Pierre asked.

"No, no," she said quickly. "You cannot sleep in a strange hotel when this house is at your disposal."

It was an unhappy evening for Miranda. The dinner she had planned with such care seemed only to emphasize her relations with Pierre as he heaped lavish praise upon each course and reminded her of past festivities of Ste. Giselle.

"You have married well, *m'sieur*,'" he told Adam. "For if all else fails you have a wife who is a chef and that oils the domestic wheels of the poorest hovel, *n'est-ce pas*?"

"Adam has never sampled my cooking before," Miranda said, and looked across at her husband for a word of praise.

Adam, who had raised his eyebrows at the Sèvres dinner service and abundance of flowers, merely said, "I had no idea you were so expert, Miranda, but was all this additional effort really necessary?"

She felt like a reproved child, and after that it was natural to turn to Pierre for all the news she was so anxious to hear.

Adam listened, watching Miranda in the candlelight and observing with brooding eyes the provocative trick she had of wrinkling her nose as she spoke and the unconscious play of her expressive hands. He was thinking of Simmy, who had smiled knowingly at the news of Pierre's arrival and had remarked, "So that explains all the fuss and festivity. Mrs. Chantry said it was a celebration—a special occasion—but of course as she had not mentioned she expected a guest, I could not understand the reason."

He had asked her on impulse to join them for coffee, not because he wanted her, but because the sight of Miranda's childish face turned to Pierre in soft oblivion of his own quiet presence might become unbearable. He watched them, and the anger still lay deep beneath his suave manner as he pictured again that lighted window and the two of them framed, as in a stage set, in each other's arms for any who cared to see.

They had their coffee in the little study and Miranda was made uncomfortable by Simmy's unexpected presence. She described at length the trouble Miranda had taken with her preparations for the evening, and when Miranda remarked rather shortly that she did not even know Pierre was in England, let alone about to visit Wintersbride, she only smiled discreetly and replied, "Well, at any rate it's nice to think your efforts were not wasted, after all, isn't it?"

Only she, thought Miranda, would notice the impertinence behind the governess's remarks; only she knew how easily Simmy's desire to spoil the evening had come about.

Pierre sought to soften matters with affectionate anecdotes of Miranda's childhood.

"She was a romantic, that one," he told Adam, shaking his head. "Always the grand passion, the single heart."

"Really?" said Adam, raising his eyebrows. "She has always insisted she was not romantic. Indeed, I understood her to say on several occasions that you had taught her that the head rules the heart—very admirable."

"O-ho!" exclaimed Pierre. "So you listened to me after all, did you, Mielle? But that is very flattering though I do not quite believe you would change so fast. Is it that *m'sieur*, too, is not romantic, and you have been married—how long? Two months only? Oh, no, *m'sieur*, that, I think, is the British reserve!"

"Very likely," remarked Adam dryly. "You are a student of psychology, perhaps?"

"I am a student of nothing, but I am French," replied Pierre airily. "I like to observe."

"You do not have to be French to do that, Mr. Morel," Miss Simms said mildly, and Miranda, wishing the conversation would change, told him a little severely not to be absurd.

He looked across at her, his eyes twinkling.

"You call me that? I know too much about you, *ma petite*, to be treated to the high English horse. You are still the little Mielle who ran barefoot over the sands with me at Ste. Giselle. Marriage has not changed you, *chérie*."

She flushed unaccountably, aware of Adam's eyes on her face, and Simmy asked if "honey" was a term of endearment in France as it was in America.

"No, no, it is a name we gave her for her coloring, you understand. A love name, you call it?"

"A nickname, I think you mean," said Simmy, glancing at Adam. "Personally, I have always thought nicknames rather silly and undignified."

"But Mielle is not dignified," Pierre retorted, unable to resist shocking the stiff English governess. "She is an *enfant terrible*, a breaker of hearts, as I should know, and her innocence is very, very misleading."

Simmy looked uneasy, but Adam said in an expressionless voice, "Yes, innocence can be misleading. Will you have some more coffee, Simmy?"

But there was no stopping Pierre, who thought it no bad thing that the stiff English husband should be made aware of his wife's charms through the eyes of a younger man.

"Innocence can also be beguiling," he said. "The freshness of youth, unspoiled, clear-eyed—is that not what all men desire? *Hélas*, youth will not wait! Did you not, Mielle, at only sixteen, promise to wait for me? But, no—you run to England and marry a gentleman much more distinguished."

Miranda's hand shook as she poured out some more coffee for herself.

"You are monstrous," she said calmly. "You know very well that was a family joke. Besides, you intended to marry Marguerite, which was very practical and quite understood. Only I think she was very sensible not to have you."

"You see—always the rap on the knuckles," Pierre said to Adam. "She never would stand any nonsense, our little Mielle."

And so it went on until Adam excused himself with his usual plea of work. Miranda looked at him with suddenly stricken eyes.

"Will you not stay for a little?" she asked.

His smile was sardonic as he replied, "I think not. You and Mr. Morel will have plenty to discuss that can be of no interest to me."

"Well," said Simmy playfully as the door closed, "I can't have you thinking I've been left as a chaperon, Mrs. Chantry, so if you will both excuse me, I will go to my room."

"That was most tactful of all concerned," observed Pierre when they were alone, but Miranda looked at him with troubled eyes.

"You should not have talked like that in front of them," she said. "Adam will not understand and the governess will make mischief."

The amusement left his face and he gave a quick frown.

"This marriage, is it not happy?" he asked.

"Oh, yes, yes. But Adam is—different. He has never, I think, learned to play as we do. He works very hard and has been alone for many years."

"But that is not right for you, my little one. You are young and should be cheerful. How is it that you choose a man with gray hairs who shuts you up in the middle of a moor and does not know how to laugh?"

"I had," said Miranda with a certain asperity, "little choice at the time. I had no money, no job and I was ill. We met by chance. Besides, you did not write and you had, I thought, made the marriage of convenience yourself."

He shot her an amused glance.

"So I set you the example and you marry the rich widower whom you say you meet by chance? You take a gamble and *voilà*, you win the lottery, my little innocent. Does that content you?"

She looked at him under her lashes.

"You have not, perhaps, allowed that I also found Adam very attractive," she said.

"So? Well that at least is good. But your husband—does he love you, *chérie*—does he make you happy?"

She sighed.

"I am at a disadvantage, you see," she said. "He was deeply in love with his first wife, and he has not yet, I think, got over her death."

"But what," asked Pierre, gently mocking, "has a dead woman got that you have not?"

"She was very beautiful," Miranda said. "Come—I will show you."

She led the way to the drawing room and switched on the lights. Pierre stood for a long time looking up at Melisande's portrait, and Miranda watched him, trying to read the expression in his face.

"Do you not agree she was beautiful!" she asked at last "As you are an artist it is a face that should appeal to you."

"As an artist there is something I do not like," he replied. "She is beautiful, yes, but it is the *beauté du diable*."

"It is strange you should say that," said Miranda slowly. "For I feel she is hostile to me—she and the house."

He laughed and pinched the lobe of her ear.

"What foolishness is this?" he exclaimed. "She is dead and her ghost cannot harm you."

"It is hard to fight a ghost," she said, and Pierre took her chin between his finger and thumb, tilting her face upward.

"Can it be that you love this strange Englishman who is so much too old for you?" he asked on a note of surprise.

"Yes, Pierre," she said with a sigh, and thought of the evening as it might have been and wished him a thousand miles away.

"That is, of course, different," he said softly, and felt her shiver.

"You are cold? You do not care for this room, naturally. Let us go," he said.

But back in the study the fire could not warm her. The rain had stopped, but mist clung to the windows and the house was silent.

"Will you mind very much, Pierre, if I go to bed?" she said. "Tomorrow we will talk, but tonight—well, I am tired."

It was early yet, and Adam, she knew, would not be up for some time. She undressed slowly, tired now with the sick, flat lassitude that came from disappointment. Before she got into bed, she opened the door between the two rooms, then lay listening to the owls and waiting.

It was late when she heard him come up, and her eyes were heavy with sleep denied. Adam stood for a moment in the doorway, and as he reached out a hand to close the door, she said, "Please come in." She switched on the light by the bed as he slowly crossed the room.

"I thought you were still downstairs with your young man," he said.

"No. I have been waiting for you for a long time," she replied, propping herself on her elbow.

"Waiting?" His voice had a curious ring. "Did you want to see me about anything, Miranda?"

"Only to say that I was so sorry Pierre should have chosen tonight."

"Tonight or any other—where's the difference?"

"Because . . . ." But she could not go on any further, and said instead, "You do not mind that Pierre is here?"

He regarded her with an odd expression.

"Is there any reason why I should mind?" he said. "Though,

since you ask me, Miranda, it would have been—usual, shall we say, to tell me he was expected.''

"But, Adam, I had no idea. Indeed, I thought that when he tapped on the window it was you.''

"Have you ever known me tap on windows?''

"N-no—but tonight was different.''

"Yes, it was, wasn't it? The Sèvres dinner service, the table decorations, and those very French dishes that you had taken so much trouble over. I've certainly never known you to be interested in cooking before.''

"But Adam, that was . . . .'' Suddenly she did not finish. If he was so blind that he could not see, if he would listen to Simmy's innuendoes and believe them, then the frail bond between them was too weak for understanding.

"I am sorry that you do not welcome my guest,'' she said, not looking at him. "But I did not invite him tonight.''

"I see. But you didn't tell me your—friendship with this young man was so close.''

"You did not ask me,'' she replied gently. "You have always had very little interest in my life before I met you, Adam.''

His mouth tightened.

"And you think that by the terms of our marriage, I should not inquire too much about old friendships?''

She looked at him under her lashes.

"Well, do you think you should?'' she said deliberately. "It is your own affair if you choose to think ill of me, Adam, but you should not be illogical. I would not make the scene if you had a *chère amie* in Plymouth, where you so often spend the night.''

"Wouldn't you, Miranda?''

"No. Me, I am logical and do not expect a man to be—to be celibate in all his habits.''

"And do you apply that to women, too?''

"Why not? It is unreasonable to ask of one what one may not of another.''

He was suddenly violently angry.

"If you're trying to tell me that you consider yourself free to amuse yourself in that sort of fashion you had better shed some of your French ideas," he said. "It may be illogical, as you like to call it—it may even be damned unfair, but whatever the terms of our marriage, I don't choose that my wife should seek consolation elsewhere. Do you understand?"

"Yes, Adam," she said and lay back on her pillows, very still. "You would not—" her voice was almost a whisper "—you would not think of—altering the terms?"

He stood looking down at her, hands thrust deep in his pockets, but there was no tenderness in his sudden smile.

"That is always possible," he said, "but in the meantime you'd better take to locking your door. Flesh and blood takes little count of contracts or obligations if tried too highly and I don't think you would care for a marriage consummated in that spirit, Miranda."

"No," she said, turning her face away from the light. "I should not care for it at all. Good night, Adam."

He stood for a moment longer, looking down at her. Anger and even jealousy were fighting against an instinct to take her in his arms, but he did not see the tears on her lashes and presently he bade her a brief good-night and went back to his room, shutting the door behind him.

CHAPTER TEN

MIRANDA was surprised to find, the next morning, that Adam had canceled his appointments for the day.

"You are staying at home?" she said, puzzled by such an unusual procedure.

"Do you object?" he asked a little ironically.

"Of course not, but—"

"This isn't a last-minute decision in order to keep an eye on your guest, you know," he said. "Unfortunately I had already made my arrangements before coming home last night."

The color crept under her pale skin, for she suddenly knew that, just as she had planned the evening as a special occasion, so had he contributed his portion and taken a day off to please her.

"What would you like to do?" she asked a little helplessly, but his smile was bitter.

"You needn't worry about me," he said. "I shall be out. I did understand Morel to say he was leaving for France today, didn't I?"

"Yes."

"And I'm sure you'd like to go and see him off."

"Yes," she said again, and was glad when he shut himself into his study.

Pierre was to sail in the afternoon so there was little time left in which to hear all the news she had longed for. It had stopped raining, but the sky was still overcast, and she and Pierre walked in the grounds, wandering down narrow, sunless alleys shadowed by high banks of rhododendrons.

Once he turned and faced her suddenly, saying with unaccustomed seriousness, "I am not happy about you, *petite*. This lonely house, these dark, dripping walks—they are not the background for you."

"They do not always drip," she replied with grave consideration. "When there is sun the garden is beautiful."

"But in this country there is not much sun. Mielle—we will not lose touch again, *hein?* Should you ever want me, I will come."

He touched her cheek with his brown fingers, and presently Miranda suggested that they return to the house.

Miranda was glad when it was time for Pierre to leave. Now that the first delight at seeing him had passed she realized that for her too much had changed since those carefree days at Ste. Giselle and there seemed nothing more to say. She would always welcome him as a link with her childhood and her father's beloved memory, but her way of life was no longer his.

It was raining again when Bidder brought the car to the door. Miranda, sitting silently beside Pierre, looked out at the sad expanse of moor and wished that she, too, had remained behind. At the pier she stood in the rain, watching the sea gulls while she waited for Pierre to go through the formalities of embarkation. There was, he told her, a delay in sailing and they might as well go on board and have some coffee. She followed him up the gangway, glad, when she got there to feel the cheerful warmth of the saloon.

"I should have married you," he said abruptly just before the last visitors' bell rang.

She tried to laugh.

"Oh, Pierre, it would never have done," she said gently. "We are alike and yet not enough alike, and I—I have found what I want even though to you it may seem strange."

"It seems to me of the strangest," he retorted with a little smile. "Well—goodbye, my little bride of winter. Do not let the frosts nip your blossoming. Goodbye. . . ."

He kissed her gently, then stood by the ship's rail and watched her small figure move out of sight down the gangway.

ADAM HAD LUNCHED with the Lathams, but he had known long before he left that it was a mistake. He should have realized that news travels fast in a village, and Grace and her mother already knew that Miranda was entertaining an attractive visitor from France. Mrs. Latham plied him with curious questions and, never noted for her tact, remarked that she had heard before there had been some young man abroad for whom the child had formed an early attachment. Did Adam think it wise to encourage these romantic friendships?

"You mustn't mind mother," Grace said when she got him alone. "She likes to believe the worst of people in the nicest possible way. Still, for all that, it's probably a good thing the young man is returning to France today. People can't help gossiping and—well, little Miranda is such a child, isn't she?"

"What you're really trying to say is that I'm far too old for her and shouldn't be surprised if she finds youth more attractive," he said bluntly.

"Well," she replied gently, "there *is* a big difference, isn't there? And then you are so little at home."

"So people have been talking anyhow, have they?"

She made a little deprecating gesture with her hands.

"But surely you must have been prepared for that," she said. "Your sudden marriage, no preparation, no honeymoon and a child you treat more as a daughter than a wife."

"Yes, I see. I suppose I must be rather blind."

She looked at him and he saw again in her eyes the stirring of that old emotion that had mainly precipitated his second marriage.

"Adam—we're such old friends. I've never understood this marriage of yours. Why did you do it?"

His answering regard was steady.

"It doesn't occur to you that I might be fond of Miranda?" he asked, and she moved impatiently.

"Oh, fond—of course you've grown fond of her, but you

didn't love her. And why, if you wanted a stepmother for Fay, did you have to choose—so unwisely? She married you for a home, Adam, not out of any sense of affection. Do you really imagine that if someone younger and more attractive comes along she won't leave you as easily as she married you?''

"Grace, please—" he said quietly, and got up. "I know you're only talking like this out of a sense of friendship, but don't, my dear. Even with you I'm not prepared to discuss all the circumstances of my marriage. I shouldn't have come here in my present mood. Forgive me and please forget such gossip as you may have heard. Rumor, you know, is very seldom true.''

He got away as soon as he could, afraid for one moment that she would be betrayed into declaring her own feelings for him. But as he drove back to Wintersbride through the rain, his thoughts were clouded with bitterness. For the gossip about his marriage he knew he had only himself to blame, but about the truth of Miranda's old attachment for Pierre he was only just beginning to wonder. By marrying her had he cheated her out of her natural right to happiness? Did she really think, as she had said last night, that it was unreasonable to demand fidelity in a marriage such as theirs?

They had been so near to fulfillment, and even if she did not love him, he thought that she had wanted him. But, watching her with Pierre and remembering that framed picture they had made in the lighted and uncurtained room, he was bitterly conscious of his own failure.

He went up to the schoolroom when he got home to see Fay. Here, too, he had failed, he thought wearily, observing the nervous, half-frightened glance the child gave him before she returned to her occupation of building a house with cards.

The child went on stacking the cards with great care and exactitude and Adam watched her. Presently Fay looked up and said with a little rush of words, ''Miranda says you can stop her doing things she wants the same as you can stop me. Stop her going to France, Adam—please stop her going to France.''

"What are you talking about, my dear? Miranda isn't going to France," he said.

"Truly?" There was doubt in the child's voice.

"Truly. When she comes home I'll tell her to come up and say good-night to you, shall I?"

"Yes, please."

He left the schoolroom with growing uneasiness and knocked on Simmy's door and asked her if she would come down to his study for a few minutes.

"Sit down, I want to talk to you," he said when she arrived. "I'm a little worried about Fay, Simmy. She seems to have a notion that Mrs. Chantry is going away. Was anything said in your hearing that could have given her that idea?"

"Oh, I think she had planned to visit her old home later on," Simmy replied lightly. "She and Mr. Morel spoke of it in front of Fay after lunch."

"I see. Do you like Mr. Morel, Simmy?"

Miss Simms hesitated. "Do you want me to be frank?" she asked.

"Naturally."

"Well, he's very charming, of course, like so many Frenchmen, but—I don't think I would altogether trust him and—I thought him a little familiar, even for an old friend."

His eyes regarded her gravely.

"Did you, Simmy?" Adam's hands, clasped before him on the desk, tightened suddenly. "People get strange notions, sometimes," he said expressionlessly. "Mr. Morel is an old friend—almost like a brother. It's perhaps natural that—strangers might get the wrong impression. I hope you'll make that clear if there should be any talk in the servants' hall, Simmy."

"But of course. Poor little Mrs. Chantry—she's been lonely. It did one good to see her pleasure. All the preparations and excitement—it was like watching a young girl getting ready to welcome her first suitor. We all noticed it, and I wish now I had not been a little sharp with her over the childish little accusation and spoiled her pleasure."

"What accusation?" Adam asked, his face hard and grim.

"Oh, just a foolish idea she had that I listened in to her telephone conversations. I would not have paid any attention, of course, if I had not been accused in front of the servants."

"What telephone conversation is this supposed to have been? I rang her myself in the morning."

"She didn't say, but later, when Mr. Morel arrived and I realized how—well—they knew each other, I had an idea she might have been talking to him and was, perhaps, a little embarrassed by the possibility of being overheard."

He leaned back in his chair, rubbing his eyes as if he was suddenly very tired.

"Yes, well, keep that idea to yourself, Simmy. We don't know that it's even true," he said. "Mrs. Chantry said, if you remember, that she had not expected Mr. Morel."

Simmy's pale eyes regarded him thoughtfully.

"Of course, it's possible," she conceded. "But then why all the preparations, the special dinner? I think, myself, that Mrs. Chantry expected the young man to dinner only and that is why no mention was made of his staying overnight. She may have thought—forgive me—that you would not approve, since it seems clear that she was fond of him in the past. They are both so very young, are they not?"

"Yes, they are very young," said Adam wearily, and looked at his watch. "Is the car not back yet? The boat should have sailed two hours ago."

"Shall I see for you?"

"No, don't bother. If they're not back in half an hour I'll call Bidder's quarters and see if there's any news. The sailings may have been delayed."

But Miranda had returned. She had slipped in quietly by the garden door and had been in time to overhear most of the end of the conversation. The door of Adam's study was ajar and it was easy to distinguish their voices. She stood, unconscious of deliberate eavesdropping, aware only of the clever plausibility of the governess's suggestions, and the bitter weariness in Adam's voice as he answered. For a moment she was tempted to confront them both and accuse Simmy to her face of mischief making, but what real explanation could she give? Simmy had admitted her remarks were based on supposition. She had only to withdraw them, leaving behind the inevitable harm she had done, and under those watchful, calculating eyes she did not care to plead for Adam's understanding. She turned instead and, fleeing silently up the stairs to her own room, flung herself on the bed and wept.

Adam was for the most part a rational man, as his calling demanded, and he did not really believe that Miranda had run away, but he admitted to relief when Bidder informed him that the car had returned nearly an hour ago, and went up to his room to change for dinner.

He stood for a moment before his dressing table, looking at the little snapshot with the curling edges, and his eye fell on Miranda's posy. It had, he supposed, been there yesterday, but in the shock of other happenings he had not noticed it. This unfamiliar attention, then, had at least been for him and not the guest, and the thought crossed his mind that Simmy could have been mistaken. He remembered his own words to Miranda on the telephone that morning. ''Shall we make it a celebration tonight?'' he had said. Miranda's preparations could well have been for him, a shy way of bidding him welcome, a wish to mark the occasion as different. He remembered his promise to bring her a present. Well, he had brought the present but had never given it to her, and on a sudden impulse he slipped the leather case containing the charming little jeweled watch he had found for her into his pocket and tried the door between their rooms. It was locked for the first and only time since he had brought her to Wintersbride, and with a chill at his heart he remembered his words of the night before, ''You'd better take to locking your door . . . flesh and blood takes little count of contracts if tried too highly . . .'' and the rest of that hard, bitter sentence.

He hesitated for a moment, then went out into the corridor and knocked on the other door of her room. At first he thought she was not there, for upon getting no reply to his knock, he

opened the door to find the curtains were already drawn and the
room was in semidarkness. Then he saw her in a huddled little
heap on the bed and he switched on the light, revealing her
distress as deliberately as he would have exposed a disease in a
patient.

She blinked painfully in the strong light and he saw the havoc
grief had made, the swollen lids, the strain about the unsteady
mouth, the defenseless unhappiness that she was too tired to
hide from him.

"You minded his going so much?" he asked.

She was too choked with tears to answer. Indeed, he doubted
very much if she had heard what he said, and although he
crossed slowly to the bed he did not touch her.

"Poor child," he said compassionately, "I should never
have married you, should I?"

She was too tired to place any other construction on his
remark save the one that he himself regretted his marriage. She
could not tell him that it was for him she wept and the whole
sorry failure of her unwanted overtures. She only thought he
looked at her with the well-disguised distaste with which he
would break the bad news to one of his patients.

"I will go away if you wish it," she said.

His eyes continued to watch her, probing, dissecting.

"Do you want to go away—back to France, perhaps?"

"If you wish," she said, and suddenly he was angry.

"No, I don't wish it," he said in a hard voice. "And I don't
think, when you come to your senses, you will wish it, either."

"I heard what Simmy was saying to you," she said. "She is
very clever at twisting the truth."

"And what is the truth, Miranda? No, perhaps you had better
not tell me. As you yourself said last night, by the terms of our
marriage I should not inquire too closely into old friendships.
Well, we'll let that pass for the present, but whatever the truth of
the matter, the fact remains there has been gossip, and although
I realize that I asked for a great deal of it by marrying so—
unsuitably—the thing is done and we must make the best of it
for the time being."

"You also think I am unsuitable?" she said in a tired voice.

"I was referring, naturally, to the difference in age," he replied smoothly. "Now—for my own shortcomings I apologize in advance. I realize that I'm too old for you, that saddling you with adult problems was hardly fair. But even so, you have a better life now than if you hadn't married me, and until such time as we can think of an alternative solution we must just go on as before. One thing, at least, need no longer trouble you. I will, of course, respect the terms of our contract to the letter. There is no need for you to lock your door in future."

She said nothing, but turned her face away from the light and his own searching regard; and presently he got to his feet.

"I'll have a tray sent up to you," he said more kindly. "I can dine alone tonight."

"Adam . . ." she said as he prepared to leave her.

"Yes?"

"I'm sorry if I have caused gossip."

"We've both caused gossip, if that's any comfort to you," he said. "We are, I fear, in the eyes of our acquaintances, an ill-assorted couple, but don't let that worry you. I rather fancy that I am the one to be censured for marrying a girl nearly young enough to be my daughter. Would you like me to mix you a sedative before you go to sleep?"

"No."

"Well, get to bed early. Good night."

ADAM REMAINED IN PLYMOUTH for the rest of the week, and she was grateful for the period of readjustment. With honest fortitude she packed away her short-lived hopes and dreams. She knew that even though he could not love her, there would come a day when he would need her, because no normal man of Adam's age, she believed, would choose to be celibate for the rest of his life. And she knew that, when that time came, she would have gathered courage enough to forget her own pride and accept what little he had to offer. In the meantime she was his guest and must make no demands upon his time and privacy.

September saw the end of summer. Miranda, staring out of

the rain-washed windows day after day, thought of the winter ahead. Winter . . . Wintersbride . . . there would be no more sunny days by the river and the garden would have lost its warmth and color. There would only be rain and drifting leaves and the silent, shuttered house.

She no longer used the drawing room, which belonged so indisputably to Melisande. She would, she thought, take over the old nursery for her own use before the winter came.

She mentioned the matter to Mrs. Yeo, who lately had seemed so much more cooperative, but the housekeeper looked doubtful.

"Well, I don't know, madam," she said. "I don't think Miss Simms would like it."

"Miss Simms? What has it got to do with her?" asked Miranda with surprise. "The room is never used."

"Well, I don't rightly know, but it was Miss Simms got Mr. Chantry to change Miss Fay over and get all that ugly modern stuff down from London. I always thought she never could abide the nursery because it used to belong to Nanny."

"Well, she is not going to lock up the nursery as she once locked up the drawing room," said Miranda.

Simmy did not openly object, but she made difficulties over what furniture could be spared from other rooms and finished by saying that she did not wish Fay to use the room.

"If I make it into my sitting room," Miranda said, "she shall certainly use it. It's a much more cheerful room than the school-room, which gets no sun."

"I think you already know why the rooms were changed," Simmy said.

Miranda replied quietly, "I know you were jealous of Nanny's influence, and I am not sure now that you were not also anxious to remove the child as far as possible from her father."

Simmy's eyebrows lifted.

"Really, Mrs. Chantry, isn't that a little fanciful?" she said. "It was Mr. Chantry himself who complained of the noise."

"What caused those screaming fits in the first place?" asked

Miranda shrewdly. But the governess only smiled a little mockingly.

"I did not frighten her into them if that is what you mean to imply," she said. "By all means use the nursery if you wish, Mrs. Chantry, but please allow Fay to remain where she's best off—in her own wing of the house."

It was difficult now, Miranda found, to get Fay to herself for any length of time. The wet weather kept them all so much indoors that it was not possible to avoid Simmy's watchful eye for long.

Miranda knew now that the governess was trying to break the child's affection for her, just as she was convinced that the same thing had somehow happened in Adam's case. Looking back on the varying incidents that had involved the little girl in dispute, Miranda began to receive a clearer and clearer impression of distortion. Although Adam always insisted that Fay could not be treated entirely as other children, was it not actually Simmy who had suggested in the first place that she was not normal? Simmy had somehow got rid of Nanny and afterward made her own rules, and it was Simmy who for so many years had fostered the child's dislike for her father by advising him not to force her affections, and by using his authority as a threat for punishment.

She tried on one occasion to talk the matter out with Adam, but he gave her rather an odd look and said, "You shouldn't try to get your own back on Simmy, Miranda. You probably misconstrued the conversation you so unfortunately overheard. She was only doing her duty, you know."

"To suggest what was not true?" she said, surprised that he had reopened the subject after so long.

"Well," he replied mildly, "true or not, I don't know that she was implying anything very wrong. I'm afraid, as she says herself, you don't care for her very much, but though she makes allowances for you, you are not so generous toward her, are you?"

Yes, thought Miranda bitterly, Simmy was expert at administering her own particular brand of poison. It was useless to try to enlist Adam's sympathy without tangible proof of guilt. Even when she quoted things that Fay had told her, he would merely raise his eyebrows and reply, as if weary of the whole subject, "My dear child, as I've told you so many times, Fay invents, but I must ask you not to encourage her by letting her think you believe her."

"I do believe her," Miranda said gravely. "I think, Adam, she is a very truthful little girl and what you have often thought were lies were not so at all."

For a moment he looked as if the idea was worthy of more careful consideration than he had given it before, then he sighed and said more patiently, "I would like to believe you, Miranda, but Simmy has known the child all her life. I must respect her experience and the evidence of my own eyes, mustn't I?"

"The evidence of your own eyes is only what Simmy has shown you, and Fay's own dislike—which, you know, Adam, is really fear, I think."

"But why should she be afraid of me? I've always tried to be patient and gentle with her."

"Yes, why should she be afraid? Because someone encourages her—because—"

"Oh, Miranda, please!" He sounded impatient again. "I hope you aren't silly enough to suggest such things to the child herself or I shall have to agree with Simmy that you aren't very good for her."

"Is that what Simmy says?" asked Miranda.

But he did not answer directly, and said instead, "Believe me, Miranda, I am not ungrateful for your interest in Fay, and I am delighted and, I admit, a little surprised that her affection for you has lasted so long. But don't, as a result, disregard Simmy. She really does know what's best."

No, thought Miranda, she would never disregard Simmy; rather, she would watch more carefully. It was plain to her that the governess was up to her old tricks of trying to wean the child away, but this time she should not succeed. Miranda's judgment was not, as Adam's had been at a critical time in his life, clouded with doubts, and she no longer believed for one moment that Fay was anything more than a perfectly normal little girl who had been the victim of too much care and supervision and the predatory instincts of a possessive woman.

As she began the first preparations for turning the old nursery into a sitting room for herself, she thought more and more about Nanny. What, wondered Miranda with increasing curiosity, had Nanny done that Adam should dismiss her so summarily a year after Melisande died?

But she did not try to talk to Adam again, and indeed there was little opportunity, for he was away a great deal. He seemed like a machine these days, unsparing of himself or his subordinates, and it was not surprising that when he came home it was simply to eat and sleep. Sometimes she watched him a little wistfully as he sat opposite her in the evenings reading or just relaxed in a chair with his eyes closed. Then he would look tired and disillusioned and rather older than his age, and she had to restrain an impulse to put out a hand and touch the graying hair with loving tenderness.

Arthur Benyon, on one of his rare visits, had told her that if Adam did not relax he would break down. Then Benyon had looked at her rather hard, as if he thought that she herself might be the cause of such preoccupation with work.

"He's taking on more and more and it's not necessary," he said gruffly. "You should get him to go for a holiday, Miranda. I can't persuade him."

"Can anyone persuade Adam to something he does not agree with?" she asked a little sadly.

"Well, you should be able to, young woman, if no one else," he replied.

He shot her a puzzled glance when she said, "I least of all."

He tackled Adam before he left.

"No man's indispensable, not even you, Adam," he said. "Miranda's beginning to look peaked, too. Take her abroad where there's some sun. Do you both good."

"A joint holiday was hardly in our itinerary," Adam said with a quirk of the lips, and was not prepared for the old man's explosive retort.

"Damn it all, man, what do you mean? You didn't have a honeymoon—well, take one now. You owe Miranda that, you know."

A honeymoon . . . what a strange, incongruous thing to owe to Miranda. His eyes were sardonic as he replied, "Do you think so?"

Benyon asked, with the bluntness of a privileged friend, "What sort of silly mess are you making of your marriage this time?"

Adam was startled. Was the strangeness of the situation so apparent to others?

"I hardly know how to answer that one, Arthur," he said a little awkwardly.

The specialist retorted, "Well, I'll answer it for you. For some reason best known to yourself, I think you've embarked on one of these highfalutin business arrangements with your wife. What's the matter with you, man? I used to think you'd fall in love with that charming little girl despite yourself. Haven't you got Melisande's poison out of your system yet?"

"Good God, long ago!"

"Well, then, what's wrong with you? And what do you imagine you're doing to Miranda?"

"You don't understand, Arthur," said Adam wearily. "And it's too long a story to go into now."

CHAPTER ELEVEN

AT THE BEGINNING OF OCTOBER, gales began to sweep across the Atlantic and Miranda had her first taste of what rough weather at Wintersbride could be like. All day and all night the wind lashed against the house and rain drove in angry squalls across the moor.

"Is it often like this?" asked Miranda, who was helping Simmy to stuff up a hole in a pane of glass that had blown in at the end of the north corridor.

"Most of the winter," Simmy replied. "We're high up here and get the full force of all the bad weather."

"It is rather eerie," Miranda said, and the governess smiled.

"You'll get used to it," she said, adding obliquely, "And if not, there's always the late Mrs. Chantry's remedy."

"Her remedy? But she was ill—she died here."

"Yes, she died here, and perhaps that's a remedy, too," said Simmy, and there was something a little frightening about the long, sallow face turned toward her in the gloom.

Miranda experienced a superstitious sense of dread. The governess, she knew, was only trying to frighten her, but what was the mysterious complaint which had kept the lovely Melisande a prisoner and finally killed her?

"Simmy—was she—was she perhaps a little mad?" she asked, her eyes wide.

Miss Simms began to sweep pieces of glass neatly into a dustpan.

"What is madness?" she said with a little smile. "Only a brain less stable than others—like little Fay's, for instance."

"You are wicked!" exclaimed Miranda, horror touching her

for a moment. "If her mother was—deranged, it does not mean that the child—"

"Doesn't it?" said Simmy, and as a gust of wind came howling down the corridor and all the lights in the house went out, Miranda turned and fled.

She sat alone in the dim library, listening to the wind, and some of her fears returned.

What had the governess been suggesting up there in the dark north corridor? Had it not been plain that she was warning Miranda of some unsuspected secret that could effect them all? So lost was she in confused reflection that she did not hear Adam come in and jumped when he suddenly spoke to her.

"Hello! Have the lights gone again?" he said, and as he saw her involuntary movement and the color drain from her face, he apologized for startling her and came to warm his hands at the fire.

"Can Bidder fix the plant tonight?" she asked.

"I should hardly think so." He glanced down at her quickly, then stooped and took her wrist between his fingers.

"Your pulse is racing," he said, looking at her more closely. "Has something upset you—or frightened you?"

Yes, she had been frightened—so frightened, she now knew, that before she could stop herself she had said, "Adam, I have never asked, but now you must please tell me—was your first wife mad?"

"Good God! What makes you ask a thing like that?" he exclaimed.

"It was Simmy," Miranda said. "She hinted that Fay—Adam, is it true? I think I have a right to know."

For a moment he did not speak and the terrible bitterness in his face made her afraid.

"No, it's not true," he said at last. "But you have, as you say, a right to he truth, Miranda. I didn't think an old, rather sad story concerned the present, but perhaps I should have explained after our dinner party, when my behavior must have seemed so strange to you."

Her mind went back to that night and she saw again the child in her long blue dressing gown, Adam, white and angry, snatching the glass of wine from her hand, and old Arthur Benyon looking on and saying, "I think you should explain your attitude, Adam."

"Oh!" she said, suddenly understanding.

"Melisande drank," he said harshly. "I brought her here, hoping to cure her, but after the first few months, we had to give out that she was ill and confine her to the house and grounds. We took every precaution, but somehow she managed to get hold of the stuff, and in the end—I don't suppose you've ever known an incurable dipsomaniac, Miranda, and I hope you never will. It's the most soul-destroying thing I know of—to have to watch, month after month, such beauty as was Melisande's disintegrate into total ruin, to see mind and willpower weaken so much that only one pitiable craving remains, and be able to do nothing."

"Oh . . . my poor Adam . . ." she said very softly, and had a poignantly vivid comprehension of what those months must have done to Adam, helpless, despite all his skill for others, to save the one woman he loved.

"Fay was sent away, of course, with Nanny, and Simmy looked after Melisande—she was used to these cases and she was fond of her. Even when she—turned against me, Simmy could always manage her."

"She, too, turned against you?"

"Oh, yes, but that's natural, you know. I was the person responsible in her eyes for denying her what she wanted. Though Simmy blamed herself at the time for the accident, it was really a merciful release."

"Oh, yes—the accident? Did she not then die here at Wintersbride?"

"No. She slipped out one day when Simmy was resting. They found her on the moor at the bottom of an old mine shaft. We'll never know if she jumped or fell, but the coroner brought in a verdict of accidental death."

"How terrible!"

"Terrible but merciful," he said sternly. "She might have lived on for years, an incurable wreck. She was my failure, Miranda."

She sat very still, wanting to take him in her arms but knowing that he was thinking only of the dead Melisande, whom he had somehow failed.

"One cannot," she said, seeking the right words, "give more than one has. You did not fail her, Adam—she could not have wanted your love enough, I think."

He looked at her then, a long, curious look, which held bitterness and regret.

"But you see," he said slowly, "I didn't love her. That was my failure."

"You didn't love her?" repeated Miranda stupidly.

He stood by the table, his profile clear and sharp against the dimmed globe of light.

"Passion is not love, Miranda—don't ever confuse them," he said, and she thought there was a hint of warning in his voice. "Melisande was brilliant and beautiful and I was very young, but passion is demanding and doesn't last. Had I loved her she might not have desired other men and, failing that, the final solace. One can't know."

She locked her hands fiercely round her knees to prevent them from reaching out to him. It was plain now what Melisande had been.

Slowly something in Miranda was released. She no longer needed to fight a dead love that had never existed, and she could not hate a poor ghost whose beauty at the end was gone. But there was still something of Melisande that could work destruction, and Miranda sprang to her feet and ran to Adam.

"Why do you stay here?" she cried urgently. "Why do you bring your child up in this—this unhappy house?"

"Don't you realize yet that I'm trying to safeguard Fay from her mother's inheritance?" he said. "Fay is her mother over again, passionate, unstable in her emotions, with the same arrogant beauty."

"No, you are wrong," Miranda said. "Adam, listen to me, I

beg you, and do not say, as you always do, that Fay invents or that I am fanciful. Simmy wishes you to think these things. She wishes to keep Fay from you. I have heard her, Adam—I have heard her suggested to Fay that you are to be feared, that you do not wish to be bothered with her. You have relied on Simmy for so long that you can no longer see that things could be different. Today, she deliberately tried to make me believe that Melisande had been—deranged, that Fay might also be affected."

He had turned up the lamp again while she was speaking, and as the light grew slowly brighter, she saw in his dark face the first signs of doubt. He put his hands on her shoulders, and his eyes searched hers, probing, demanding.

"Do you realize what you are accusing her of?" he asked.

"Yes," she replied, her eyes clear and steady. "Simmy wants power. She is possessive and sees her position threatened with each fresh move you make. If the child loves you she will be normal with you, if she is treated like other children she will prove to be just as they are. Your second marriage has already threatened her authority, though she has done her best to treat me always as a child. If Fay grew up as she should, going to school, making friends that took her away from here, what would Simmy's position be? She would leave when the time came and her services were no longer needed. But as things are, she is here for life if she is clever, so she cannot afford to miss a single chance of asserting her authority or of making mischief. I do beg of you, Adam, to think about what I have said and to observe for yourself. Do you not see that it is possible you have been wrong—that in your daughter you may have the answer to what you think of as your failure?"

She felt his fingers grip her shoulders, and his voice was suddenly harsh as he replied, "If I thought you were right," he said. "If I thought there was the smallest chance you could be right . . . but Simmy . . . it sounds incredible. . . ."

"Think back, Adam. Was Fay an ordinary, natural child all the time Nanny had her?"

"Yes. I didn't see a great deal of her, of course, while her mother was ill, but later—she was very fond of Nanny, you know. I'm afraid Nanny's going was the cause of the child's dislike for me.''

"Why did you dismiss her?"

"His hands dropped from her shoulders and he turned away.

"We discovered she had been responsible for bringing drink into the house. She wasn't entirely to blame, I suppose. Melisande had always been able to get around her, and she was uneducated and obstinate and probably didn't realize the harm she was doing. But of course I couldn't keep her on for Fay.''

Miranda wrinkled her forehead.

"And this was a whole year after your wife died? Was that not rather strange?''

"Not really. Simmy had known for some time but didn't want to distress me. It was only when the time came for her to leave herself that she thought I ought to know Nanny wasn't altogether trustworthy.''

Miranda's silence made him turn to look at her again, and something in her face made him exclaim quickly, "But that's unthinkable!''

"Is it?" said Miranda gently. "But do you not consider it rather strange that Simmy should wait until she is to go herself to accuse Nanny?''

"No—no, certainly not. She was concerned for the child when she should no longer be here herself.''

"So you asked her to stay on instead of Nanny, and she accepted at once?''

"Not at once. She had little experience of governessing, then.'' He rubbed his eyes wearily with the backs of his knuckles. "I think perhaps we are both a little fogged and out of focus, my dear. This gale gets on one's nerves, doesn't it? Perhaps one day I'll take your advice and get rid of Wintersbride.''

"And you'll listen to me now without—without impatience?''

"Am I impatient with you? Yes, I'm afraid I often am. Yes, I'll listen, Miranda, and now that you know a little more about me perhaps you'll bear with my moods.''

He put a hand under her chin, tilting her face to the light.

"You don't look well," he said. "Perhaps I ought to send you away for a bit."

"So I was telling Mrs. Chantry a little earlier," said Simmy's voice from the doorway. As usual she had entered the room so quietly that neither of them had heard her, and Miranda wondered how long she had been standing there.

"You think she should go away, Simmy?" Adam asked, a curious inflection in his voice.

He was regarding her with a strange expression, as if he was seeing her for the first time, and her glance went quickly to Miranda's flushed face.

"A break is always a wise precaution when nerves are a little frayed," she replied in her colorless voice. "Too long cooped up in one place makes us—overimaginative, don't you think?"

"Perhaps," he said noncommittally, and she smiled.

"I only came to see if you had forgotten the time, as I did not hear you come up to change," she said. "It's half-past seven."

Adam frowned, for the first time irritated by her interruption.

"Then we won't bother to change at all," he said a little brusquely. "Don't trouble to remind us another time, Simmy. Dinner won't be kept waiting."

The shadows were too deep for the expression on her face to be read, but Miranda saw her hands move quickly at her sides.

"Very well. I'm sorry for disturbing you," she said quietly, and left the room.

FOR SEVERAL DAYS after that, Simmy kept Fay in her own wing, saying that she had a slight cold. It was an excuse to keep her away, Miranda thought, but by the end of the week the girl from the village went down with influenza, and a few days later Mrs. Yeo and Bessie succumbed.

Miranda and Nancy took over the house between them, Miranda turning cook with much satisfaction while Nancy ran up and down to the sickrooms with trays. Simmy declined to take over such little nursing as was necessary, saying that she could not run the risk of carrying the infection to Fay, but Nancy was of the opinion that the governess thought it beneath her to wait on servants. And while she looked after Bessie, Miranda thought it only tactful to minister to Mrs. Yeo herself.

"You oughtn't to be doing this at all, Miranda," Adam told her. "It would have been very much better if Simmy had taken on the nursing and let you look after Fay."

"She did not think so when I suggested it," said Miranda, and he gave her a quick look.

"Have you see Fay lately?"

"Oh, no, because, you see, now I am in direct contact and Simmy will not permit visits to the schoolroom."

"I see. Well there's no reason why you shouldn't meet in the open air. A brisk walk would do you both good. I'll speak to Simmy," he said, and Miranda knew that he was displeased by the governess's attitude.

So now, each morning if the weather was fine, Fay and Miranda took a walk together. The child delighted in being excused from lessons and was much surprised that it should be her father who had ordered the change.

"Simmy said it was Adam who wouldn't let me see you," she told Miranda, "but I heard him tell her I was to stop lessons for the time being and go out with you alone whenever I liked, so Simmy must have got it wrong, mustn't she?"

"Yes, my cabbage, Simmy gets many things wrong," Miranda answered. "I have always told you that your father wants you to be happy, but he does not get a chance of knowing what you want if you do not tell him."

"I suppose not, but Simmy always said I wasn't to bother him. Do you think, Miranda, he would come for a walk with us on the weekend?"

Miranda's heart lifted. It was the first time she had ever known the child express a tentative wish for her father's company.

"I'm sure that he will," she said warmly, and prayed very earnestly for a fine Sunday.

It was an illuminating walk for Adam. Once free of her initial awkwardness, Fay chattered away, letting fall innocent remarks that set him thinking. He watched her with Miranda, and could not deny that the spontaneous affection with which she treated the girl had all the appearance of the natural devotion of a warmhearted little girl. He, like Miranda, no longer believed that this was one of the emotional instabilities that Simmy was always guarding against, and when, during the homeward walk, the child without hesitation slipped a hand into his, he gave it a grateful squeeze and smiled down at her in such a way as to receive a half shy, half surprised smile in return.

Miranda enjoyed her hours in the kitchen preparing the food while she listened to Nancy's gossip. She took special delight in cooking tempting meals for Mrs. Yeo.

"I would like to say, madam, that I very much appreciate all the trouble you have gone to," Mrs. Yeo said the day before she was to get up for the first time. "Not many would have done as you have, not even, God forgive me, my other dear lady, for she was not one to think of others, poor soul."

Miranda, touched at now being bracketed approvingly with Melisande's well-loved name, said gently, "Perhaps she could not think of others, Mrs. Yeo. When someone is as sick as she was, the mind is not responsible."

"That's both true and charitable," Mrs. Yeo said, nodding her head. Then she asked, a little sharply, "Did Miss Simms tell you what was the matter with Mrs. Chantry?"

"No, Mr. Chantry told me."

"That's right. Don't let Miss Simms acquaint you with facts that you ought to know. She has an ugly tongue."

Miranda sat down on the bed.

"Mrs. Yeo, you knew Nanny well," she said. "Do *you* think her dismissal was right?"

An unaccustomed flush stained the housekeeper's flat cheeks. For a moment she pursed her lips, as if she was forcing back an unguarded word then she said with slow deliberation, "No, madam, I do not, but you are the first to ask me that and I would like to know what made you ask."

"Because," said Miranda, a little pulse of excitement beginning to throb in her temple, "I think the evidence came only from Miss Simms, and I think Miss Simms had reason to wish Nanny out of the house with no hope of returning."

Mrs. Yeo took a deep breath, then felt blindly for one of Miranda's hands.

"You're right, madam," she said, the flush deepening. "And so I told the master at the time. But, poor gentleman, he had been through so much. He wouldn't listen to servants' gossip, he said. We all resented Miss Simms, he said, because of her position in the house, but he had reason to trust and be grateful to her and he only wanted to do the best for his little girl. I don't rightly know how Miss Simms found the evidence that convinced the master, but Nanny swore till the day she left that nothing had been in those bottles but her own cowslip wine, which wouldn't hurt a fly. She used to give it to my poor lady watered down with sugar when the craving came over her, and all it could possibly do was to give her the comfort of a glass in her hand, if you understand my meaning."

"And what happened to Nanny?"

Mrs. Yeo looked surprised.

"She's only ten miles away the other side of the moor, where she was born," she said. "Retired she is and living on her brother's farm these last five years. She writes to me regular for news of Miss Fay."

"Would she talk to me, do you think, if I went to see her?"

Mrs. Yeo considered the question, looking at Miranda a little dubiously.

"Well, as to that I don't know. It was all so long ago and it's best to let sleeping dogs lie," she said.

"Mrs. Yeo," Miranda said carefully, "I have reason to think, and so I believe have you, that Miss Simms has caused a great deal of trouble in this house. I trust you, so I will tell you that I believe she has come between Miss Fay and her father by making out that the child is—different from other children. I know that many of the inventions and supposed falsehoods that Miss Fay is credited with have been put into her head by Miss Simms herself. I must be able to *prove* the truth to Mr. Chantry, for he has trusted Miss Simms for so long that he is not easy to convince. Is it not better that I see Nanny, who is perhaps the one person who really knows?''

A strange expression crossed the housekeeper's face as she spoke and her little bright eyes watched Miranda closely.

''You have a wise head on you, for all your childish appearances, my dear,'' she said. ''Go and see Nanny. I will give you her address.''

It was not possible, however, to go at once. With only Nancy and herself to run the house between them, Miranda found little time for visiting.

With both Mrs. Yeo and Bessie sick, Adam and Miranda dined in the small study and waited on themselves. Miranda enjoyed the informal meals, delighting in surprising Adam with a new dish and relating the trivial happenings of the day with a turn of phrase that could usually make him laugh. At moments she could pretend to herself that the bitter words that had passed between them on the occasion of Pierre's visit had not been said, and she would find him watching her with eyes that at times were puzzled, and at others unexpectedly tender. He no longer shut himself up in his own study after dinner, but seemed content to remain with her by the fire. And she would observe with satisfaction the tiredness leaving his face as his body slowly relaxed in the big chair.

But the evening was always over once bedtime came and they left the friendly warmth of the study. Although she had long ago unlocked the door again between their rooms, he never used it. Their good-nights were said in the chilly corridor and she had not the courage to find an excuse to invite him in. Once, to postpone the moment of separation, she took him into the nursery to describe her plans for turning it into a sitting room for herself.

''Why have you chosen this room?'' he asked, picking up one of the wooden animals that still stood on the mantelpiece and turning it over idly in his hands.

''It is convenient,'' she said glibly, unable to tell him that for her the nursery would form a link with him and, by reason of its proper designation, one day he might desire more of her. "It is on the same floor as my bedroom and is sunny and never used. Besides, I like nurseries."

"Do you, Miranda?" he said, giving her a very odd look.

For a moment she thought he was going to add something further. But he apparently changed his mind and, bidding her a brief good-night, went on to his own room.

BY THE BEGINNING OF NOVEMBER the house had returned to its usual routine.

Tonight, the first for a week after the house was back to normal, Miranda sat listening absently while Simmy discussed some point in Fay's timetable with Adam. She was thinking that now that she had leisure again, she must make that journey across the moor to see Nanny. If it was a fine day tomorrow she might go then.

"I'm sorry, Simmy," she said, realizing the governess had spoken to her. "What did you say?"

"I said I had found one of those girls' school stories you left for Fay under her pillow this morning," Miss Simms repeated, and Miranda smiled. So Nancy's novelettes had been discarded for more wholesome literature!

"I was just telling Mr. Chantry that I thought such reading was a little unsuitable as there is no question of Fay ever going to school," Simmy said.

Before Miranda could reply, Adam said pleasantly, "I've been reconsidering that matter, Simmy, and I'm not at all sure a carefully selected school of the right type mightn't be a good plan for the child when she's older."

Miranda looked at him quickly. Was he really serious or was he testing Simmy's reaction for his own or Miranda's benefit? The governess was too quick with her reply.

"You know that it's out of the question, Mr. Chantry," she said, and Adam's eyebrows went up swiftly.

"I know you've always thought so, Simmy, but you could be wrong," he answered.

Miss Simms shot Miranda a vindictive glance.

"I've no doubt Mrs. Chantry has been talking to you," she said. "But, forgive me, she does not understand the position as you and I do."

"Well, I don't know," said Adam, pushing back his chair in order to watch the two of them. "Mrs. Chantry is young and possibly has clearer judgment, and I must own I find nothing delicate in Fay, either physically or—mentally—today."

If it was a deliberate challenge, Simmy rushed unthinkingly to meet it.

"You do not see her as I do," she said. "Even Mrs. Chantry does not understand that the child she knows is quite different from the child I have to deal with. Those nights of bad dreams, the hysterical outbursts, the moods that are kept only for me because in the schoolroom there is no one else to see or hear. School is for normal children, not ones such as Fay."

Miranda sat very still, watching Adam's face, which, expressionless until the end of Simmy's outburst, suddenly froze into icy hardness.

"I have had little evidence that Fay is not normal for some time," he said quietly.

The governess looked frightened.

"But you've always said yourself—" she began.

"I should like to think we were both mistaken in some of the things that have been said—or suggested," Adam interrupted suavely. "Perhaps it hasn't occurred to either of us that if you are the person most treated to these scenes that might point to the fact that it would possibly be better if the child was not left so exclusively in your charge."

The slow, difficult color mounted under Miss Simms's sallow skin, and for a dismayed moment Miranda thought the governess was going to cry.

"Are you trying to tell me that you want me to go?" she asked.

"Of course not, Simmy. I was only suggesting that more freedom from the schoolroom might be a good thing now that the child is older. It's time you took a holiday, you know. I'm afraid I'm apt to forget how long you've been here without a break. Think about a couple of weeks of being away, will you, Simmy? Mrs. Chantry can look after Fay while you're gone.''

Simmy veiled her eyes.

''It would not do for me to go for so long,'' she said colorlessly. ''A night or two, perhaps, but that can wait. Now, if you will excuse me, I have things to do.''

The room seemed very quiet after she had gone. Miranda, her eyes on her empty coffee cup, waited for Adam to speak.

''Well?'' she said as the silence grew.

Adam's face was expressionless.

''Well, it's evident she needs a holiday,'' he observed. ''But whether you or I or anyone else will persuade her to go is another matter. Come along, my dear, the room's getting cold.''

Yes, thought Miranda, as he stood aside to allow her to pass, tomorrow, wet or fine, she must visit Nanny.

The morning was dry but overcast. Mist hung about the moor, already white and thick in the hollows, as the little country bus carried Miranda along the winding road that crossed ten miles of Dartmoor.

It seemed a long way, but at last Miranda was set down at the crossroads and the way to the farm was pointed out to her before the bus drove on and she was alone. The farm, when she reached it, looked as lonely and shuttered as Wintersbride, and for a moment she was afraid. Would Nanny talk after all these years, or was she perhaps as gray and secret as the house, resentful of strangers like so many country people?

Miranda walked down the rough, stony path to the open yard gate, and met a man coming from the barn carrying a pail of milk in each hand.

''Could I see Miss Coker?'' she asked.

The man set down his milk pails and looked at her suspiciously.

''Her won't go out to oblige, and so I tells 'em all,'' he said discouragingly. ''Her's got a home now and no need to mind other folk's children and break her heart over 'em, too.''

''I did not want to see her on business,'' Miranda said,

smiling at him placatingly. "I do very much want to see her, but it is just a friendly call."

"Ar! Happen you'm one of her nurslings, eh?" he replied with an unexpected grin. "They do come time to time, but they forget as they grow up, her always says. Come round to the back, miss, reckon we'll find 'ee in the kitchen."

She followed him across the yard to the back of the house, and he pushed open a door, shouting, "Sis—here's a visitor for 'ee! Who did you say you was, m'dear?"

"I'm Mrs. Chantry," said Miranda shyly.

As the door was suddenly flung wide from within, a woman's voice exclaimed, "Oh, my dear soul!"

Miranda stood on the threshold and sensed herself being watched by two pairs of eyes. She could not see the woman who had spoken for she stood back in the shadows, but the man said on a harsh note, "Chantry!" and made as if to close the door in her face.

" 'Tes all right, Tom," the woman said in her soft west-country voice. "For a moment I thought—but of course you'm the new lady over to Wintersbride. Come in and let us see you, m'dear."

Miranda came slowly into the low-ceilinged kitchen. She stood before Nanny, of whom she had thought so long and so much, and her disquiet vanished. Ellen Coker was a round, pink little woman with frizzy gray hair and bright, kindly eyes that looked, too, as if they could be stern if need be. Her cheeks were puckered, though she was not really old, but the skin was soft and as rosy as an apple.

"Oh, my! You'm nothing but a little girl!" she exclaimed, her eyes opening wide with surprise. "I did hear tell the new Mrs. Chantry was a surprise to the neighborhood, but you—well, whatever was the master thinking of!"

Miranda smiled a little forlornly.

"I'm afraid my youth has been a great disadvantage all round," she said, and Ellen Coker's eyes softened.

"Never you think it, m'dear," she said. "We all grow old quick enough, and though I won't deny you gave me a turn, that's only because Wintersbride is no fit place for young folks, in my opinion. But what am I thinking of, keeping you standing in the draft, ma'am! Come you in and sit by the fire and I'll find 'ee a pastie and a cup of tea. Go along about your work, Tom. The young lady and I'll want to talk private.''

The man hesitated. Wintersbride was clearly a name that did not please him, but after another nod from his sister he went out and closed the door.

''Now,'' said Nanny, ''take off your coat or you won't notice the comfort of it when you go out again, and give me some news of my little Miss Fay. Did she send her love to her old Nanny or has she been taught to forget me?''

Miranda sat down on a low stool by the big open range.

''No one knew I was coming,'' she said gently. ''But I am sure that Fay would wish to send her love. She speaks of you still.''

''Well,'' said Nanny, when they were settled over the fire with their cups of tea, ''you didn't come all the way across the moor by bus to talk nonsense to Nanny Coker, did you, m'dear? What made you come to see me? Not *her*, I'll be bound! She'd have stopped you some ways had she known.''

''Miss Simms? Why should she stop me?''

But Nanny only smiled. The first move was not going to come from her.

Miranda sipped her tea. There was so much to say and no beginning and no end, and Nanny, if she knew why Miranda had come, might simply think her prying. Her eye fell on a tall bottle with a label standing on the dresser.

''So you still make cowslip wine,'' she said.

Nanny's eyes regarded her gravely.

''Is that what you'm come about?'' she asked sternly. ''To gossip over an old scandal?''

Miranda put down her cup and saucer and clasped her thin hands round her knees, leaning forward into the circle of fire-light.

''No,'' she said, ''I have come to ask for the truth as I think only you can tell it.''

For a moment the rosy face twisted in a grimace of distaste. "Won't the master have told you that?" she said.

"He has told me what he believes is the truth, but it is Simmy's version, not his. Nanny—" Miranda lifted her face like a pleading child "—I am not curious about the past—until the other day I knew nothing—but I love Fay and I have seen very clearly now what that woman is trying to do. If you will not help me I can never make my husband understand."

Nanny reached for one of her brother's socks and began to complete a half-finished darn.

"You can see the truth when others cannot?" she murmured.

"Yes, because I have not got both feet buried in the past," Miranda replied sturdily. Ellen Coker smiled, then her eyes were grave again as she asked if Miranda knew why she had been dismissed.

"Yes, but, Nanny, do you not see that is not important now?" Miranda said. "What is important is the part Miss Simms played, for do you not see that it was all deliberate? Until she thought she would have to leave Wintersbride she said nothing. Why should she say nothing of something so serious for a whole year? It is to me proof that she is lying."

"She said nothing, m'dear, because it was she who had been found out before ever the master heard a different tale," said Nanny a little grimly.

"What do you mean? That it was really she who gave in to Mrs. Chantry's failing and you found her out?"

"Yes, m'dear, that's right. I'd had my suspicions for a brave little while and one day I caught her red-handed. It was only two days before the poor mistress died and afterward she got me to promise I would say nothing as she would be leaving the place. Well, I agreed, for the knowledge could do the master no good now. Well, she stayed on and on until I myself gave the master a hint that there was no work for her now at Wintersbride and she was upsetting the servants giving orders as if she was mistress here. Then quick as knife she turns the tables on me. She discovers one of my old cowslip wine bottles and declares it smells of gin, which it does. I can't deny, you see, taking those bottles in to the mistress from time to time, for the servants have seen me.''

''But did you not deny it was anything stronger?'' asked Miranda.

Nanny paused in her darning and her eyes were a little bitter.

''Yes, I denied it,'' she said slowly. ''But to tell you the truth, Mrs. Chantry, ma'am, I was too much hurt to put up much of a fight. It wasn't until long afterward that I understood that the strain the master had been under had caused him to act as he never would have done had he been in his right senses, though, mind you, if I had known that Miss Simms was going to stop on and take my place with Miss Fay, I'd have put up a proper show. Ah, well, it's all past and done with and now that you know the truth, I don't see how it can help you.''

''It will at least help me if, should I ask you, you will agree to tell this story again to my husband,'' Miranda said. ''Did you accuse Simmy when she accused you?''

The darning needle flashed in the firelight as Nanny wove it neatly in and out of the wool.

''No,'' she said without looking up. ''What was the use? It would have looked as if I was just an ignorant countrywoman trying to shift the blame onto someone else. It doesn't matter now.''

Miranda was suddenly kneeling on the floor beside her chair.

''But, Nanny, it matters what happens to Fay—it matters that her father's affection should be kept from her and that he should believe what is not true about her. Nanny—Fay was a normal little girl all the time you looked after her, was she not?''

''My little Miss Fay? Whatever makes you ask a thing like that?''

''Because her father imagines her to be—different from other children. Was she—affectionate toward him?''

''Yes, indeed, when he had the time to spare for her. Of course when Mrs. Chantry was bad I had to take her away for a time, but afterward—well, I reckoned the poor gentleman was getting the love and comfort the other one denied him. But why

lo you ask these things, m'dear? I hear from Emily Yeo once in
a while and she tells me my little girl is well and growing very
bonny.''

"Mrs. Yeo would not wish to make trouble. Her position
with Miss Simms is, no doubt, difficult,'' said Miranda. "Listen, Nanny, while I tell you what I think is happening and see if
you do not agree we must find some way of opening my
husband's eyes.''

"You'm right, m'dear. Things aren't as they should be from
what you tell me. Children do, of course, have funny notions,
turning against those they love and the like, but there's always a
reason and it never lasts. What will you do, now?''

"I do not know," Miranda replied, trying to think clearly.
"But I think Simmy is getting careless. After last night she will
begin to fear for her position because at last Adam is not so sure
of her. She may make a mistake—I do not know. But if the time
does come, I must have your promise, Nanny, that you will
come forward with the true story, for the child's sake—and
perhaps for mine, for she has harmed me, too.''

"I promise," said Nanny, and suddenly Miranda found she
was weeping against that crisp starched apron while Nanny's
arms went around her.

"There, m'dear, you'm better for tears like all unhappy
children. There's too much on your shoulders and that's the
truth. Can't you go to your husband, child, when you want to
weep? Is he too busy or too hard to understand?''

"He does not love me," said Miranda.

"Well, that's as maybe, but he didn't love that other one, you
know. Don't 'ee let that poor soul stand between you. You'm
what he needs now the rest is forgotten—you and some young
ones to make up for all he's missed.''

No wonder Fay had loved Nanny Coker, Miranda thought,
drying her eyes, and no wonder Simmy had feared her.

"Nanny," she said, beginning to put on her coat and scarf,
"if it became possible—and we asked you very humbly—
would you come back to Wintersbride?''

"Yes, m'dear, I'd come," said Ellen Coker. "And when you have babies of your own, perhaps old Nanny will be wanted again. Now we mustn't stop here chittering or you'll miss the bus. My, the mist's coming in thick! I'll walk with you to the crossroads to see you don't get lost."

CHAPTER TWELVE

THE BUS was slow returning, for the visibility was poor. Miranda sat watching the swirling fog that hid all but the nearest landmarks and wondered how she could best use her knowledge. Adam, she knew, was beginning to consider the governess in a new light, but it was not enough to offer Nanny's evidence after so long and it might only annoy him that she had taken it upon herself to discuss his affairs with a servant whom he had once dismissed. But Simmy must go—of that Miranda was convinced—for the child's sake and for Adam's and even perhaps for her own, for the woman would make mischief whenever she could.

When she reached the gates of Wintersbride she was surprised to see Adam coming down the driveway to meet her.

"Is that you, Miranda?" he called at once, and his voice sounded sharp and anxious.

"My dear child!" he said when he had reached her. "Never go away from the house on a day like this without saying where you're going."

"I'm sorry," she said. "But of course I did not think you would be home."

"That's beside the point. If anything should happen no one would know where to find you."

Her imagination, already overstimulated by the events of the morning, made her misunderstand him.

"Has anything happened?" she asked, fear in her voice.

The harshness left his face and he looked down at her with a puzzled expression.

"No, of course," he said. "I meant if anything happened to you. Don't do it again, will you?"

"Very well. Why are you home, Adam?"

"Canceled appointments. You don't sound very pleased. Have I broken up some secret assignation?"

He spoke teasingly, aware of the unusual tension in her thin little face. But on seeing the startled look she gave him he put a reassuring hand on her shoulder.

"I'm not serious, you know," he said. "Where have you been?"

"To see Nanny," she replied a little defiantly, but he only looked puzzled.

"Do you mean Nanny Coker, who used to be here?" he asked. "But I'd no idea she was anywhere in the district."

"But, Adam, did you not know she was living with her brother at Sowton Farm across the moor?"

He looked surprised.

"I knew, of course, there was a brother—I believe all the Cokers were born at Sowton—but I imagined Nanny was in another job somewhere."

"She's been there for five years," said Miranda slowly. "She writes to Mrs. Yeo regularly. Simmy must have known."

He gave her a quick glance.

"Well, I suppose there's no reason why she should have told me if she did know. How was Nanny looking? Sometimes, you know, I have the feeling I may have misjudged her a little. I don't think she would have deliberately betrayed a trust."

"You did misjudge her," said Miranda.

The whole matter became suddenly vitally urgent, and all thoughts of the wisest course to take left her as she looked up into his dark, faintly troubled face. "You should go and see Nanny. Adam, I beg you to go and see her and hear from her what she has told me. You have been blind all these years, for you should have listened to Nanny and not to that other."

For a moment he was strangely moved. There was a truth in Miranda that could not be denied.

"Well, we can't stand out here in the damp discussing past history," he said. "Come back to the library fire."

They walked in silence to the house. Adam had left the front door open and as she entered the hall ahead of him Miranda heard voices coming from the library.

"So you come down here to read forbidden books, do you?" the governess was saying. "I've told you before, Fay, dear, that the sort of school you will be sent to, if you are so foolish as to ask to go, is not at all like the schools in these trashy stories. You don't want to go away to school, do you, dear? You'll tell your father that you'll always want to stay at Wintersbride with Simmy?"

Adam, with a quick frown, was already on his way to the open door of the library, but Miranda put a hand on his arm.

"Wait," she whispered.

"I do want to go to school," Fay was saying. "I would have other children to play with and Miranda says I could bring friends home for holidays. I've never had a friend, Simmy, except Miranda."

"She is not your friend, dear," Simmy said clearly. "She wants to get rid of you like your father does. She doesn't care for you, Fay, any more than your father did."

Adam made an involuntary movement but Miranda held him back. Simmy's voice went on and on. "Do you know the sort of school they are planning to send you to? It's called a reform school and looks like Princetown Prison, as I told you once before. You wouldn't want to go to a place like that, would you? I can save you, you know, as long as you always make it plain you want me to stay at Wintersbride."

"I don't believe you!" Fay was frightened but not quite defeated. "Why should they want to send me to a horrid place like that?"

"Because," said Simmy, her voice suddenly venomous, "you are like your mother. You have her bad blood in you and if you don't want to be locked up in a place where you will be forgotten, you must remember that only I can prevent it. As long as I'm here you are safe, but—"

Adam shook himself free, and his voice was like the crack of a whip as he spoke the governess's name from the doorway.

Miss Simms wheeled around to face him. There was fear and bitter chagrin in her face before she said, quickly, "Oh, Mr. Chantry, I didn't know you were back. I was just telling Fay—"

"I heard most of what you were telling Fay," said Adam, and the anger in his voice made even Miranda flinch.

The child ran past her father into Miranda's arms.

"It's not true, it's not true what she said, is it?" she said, beginning to cry.

"No, my rabbit," soothed Miranda. "She is not well, *chérie*—she does not know what she is saying. Go now to Mrs. Yeo in the kitchen and stay there until I come. Dry your eyes, *petite*, everything will be all right."

Fay ran across the hall and pushed her way through the green baize door, leaving a tense silence behind her. Adam did not move.

"You will pack and be out of this house by tonight," he said then, in tones of ice.

"Won't you let me explain?" Simmy said, beginning to twist her hands together. Her pale eyes looked everywhere but at Adam. "You wouldn't dismiss me without a fair hearing, would you, Mr. Chantry?"

Adam listened, his eyes like flint.

"Did Nanny Coker get a fair hearing?" asked Miranda, and Simmy rounded on her.

"Nanny got what she deserved. She had every chance to explain and she didn't take it."

"Because it would only have looked blacker for her to accuse the accuser, and because she was hurt at being disbelieved."

"How do you know so much about the supposed feelings of a woman you have never met?" the governess demanded scornfully, and Adam placed a silencing hand on Miranda's arm.

"It doesn't matter now. I would rather you left us, Miranda. What I have to say is best said in private."

She shook his hand off.

"No, Adam, this is important and matters to quite a few

people. I have just come from seeing Nanny, Simmy. You did not wish us to know she lived so close, did you? She has told me the truth. It was you who encouraged Mrs. Chantry's failing, was it not? It was you who afterward put gin dregs in Nanny's empty wine bottles and produced them as evidence of Nanny's guilt one year later.''

"Is this true, Miranda?'' asked Adam sharply, and his face was white with the effort to control himself.

"Nanny has never lied from that day to this,'' said Miranda. "Or, indeed, I should think, in her whole life.''

The governess was breathing heavily and her eyes had a cornered look.

"You're mad, Mrs. Chantry,'' she said, trying to speak rationally. "You always have been fanciful, haven't you?''

"This is not fancy,'' said Miranda.

"No? Well, it's not fact, as any lawyer would tell you. Can you prove your case, Mrs. Chantry?''

Something had been worrying Miranda all along since her talk with Nanny, some trivial detail that did not fit. Now her mind opened out in a flood of light as she remembered the teachings of her father.

"Yes, I think I can,'' she said slowly. "If those bottles had been standing empty for a year the dregs would have lost their bouquet, for gin does not mature, and the strength would be gone. The dregs in those bottles must have been fresh—put there when they were found. Am I not right, Adam?''

For a moment, sheer surprise drove the sternness from his face as he answered gravely, "Perfectly right. I should have thought of it at the time.''

"You little bitch!'' the governess said between her teeth, and as she made a movement toward Miranda, Adam caught her wrists in his strong surgeon's hands, holding her helpless.

"That's enough,'' he said, his face suddenly like granite. "Miranda, will you please leave us now? You've proved your case, I think, beyond dispute. Thank you. The rest is left for me to deal with.''

Miranda went. Now that it was over she felt curiously weak,

and when she got to the kitchen to fetch Fay, Mrs. Yeo took one look at her and pushed her into her own vast wicker chair.

"A little drop of brandy, now, madam. You look quite white," she said, and unlocked her private cupboard, which held luxuries not permitted for general use.

"Are there to be changes, madam?" she asked, one eye on Fay.

"Yes," said Miranda. "At once, I think."

"What changes?" asked Fay, who was happily eating raisins and seemed to have forgotten her earlier fright.

"Simmy will be going, *chérie*."

"For good?"

"Yes, for good. Shall you mind?"

"I don't think so. Will Nanny côme back?"

Miranda smiled across at her.

"Would you like that?" she asked.

The child stopped munching raisins and a strange look of serenity came over her face.

"I can't remember her awfully well, but she was kind and soft and nice to cuddle, wasn't she? Yes, I should like her to come back."

"Then, my cabbage, I think she will," Miranda said. "It will all be as it once was with Nanny and your father to love and perhaps spoil you a little. Only now, of course, there is Miranda, too."

"Darling Miranda . . . I'm so glad Adam married you and not Grace . . ." said Fay.

Miranda was beginning to wonder how Adam was dealing with Simmy when he came into the kitchen.

"Mrs. Yeo, could you—" he began, and glanced at Fay.

"Run into the servants' hall, love," the housekeeper told the child. "Bessie's out but Nancy will play a game with you."

"What has happened?" asked Miranda. He looked tired and a little grim but his voice had lost some of its harshness.

"She's packing," he said briefly. "But I'd sooner she wasn't left alone for too long. I'd like you to go up, officially to lend a hand, Mrs. Yeo, and stay with her till she's ready to leave. Bidder is bringing the car around in twenty minutes.''

"Yes, sir, I understand." Mrs. Yeo left the kitchen at once and went upstairs.

"How—how does she seem, Adam?" Miranda asked.

"Quite quiet. I don't think there will be any trouble, but with a woman of that sort it's best not to take any chances. Miranda—" He pulled her out of Mrs. Yeo's big chair, and drew her hands against his breast. "I owe you both an apology and a debt of gratitude I shall never be able to repay. Can you forgive me for being so blind—so easygoing? If it wasn't for you, my gallant little crusader, I might have continued in my cross folly for the rest of my life.''

"No, Adam, you would not," she said gently. "One day when—if you saw me as a woman and not as a child, you would have listened to me, I think.''

His eyes were suddenly sad.

"Have I never listened to you?" he asked.

"Once, I thought—but you have never wanted anything of me, Adam, have you?''

For a moment his eyes were bright and demanding.

"So you think that, do you? Perhaps I'm not the only blind mouse in the family," he said with a little quirk of wry amusement. "I think, my dear, we shall have to have a thorough spring-cleaning all around at Wintersbride.''

"But spring is far away," said Miranda, so near to tears that she could only think literally, "and you never, Adam, clean house before winter is over.''

"We'll see," he said, giving her a long, searching look that made her glance away, and released her hands as Bidder entered by the back door to say the car was waiting at the front of the house.

When the two men had gone, Miranda sat alone, listening to the kitchen clock's loud tick and reviewing her own tired thoughts. Had he been apologizing to her because he had not wanted what she had once offered? Did he not understand that he owed her nothing that could not be given freely? Was she still for him a child of whom he had perhaps grown fond because his own child had wanted none of him?

She closed her eyes. Sleep and forgetfulness were very near when Mrs. Yeo came back into the kitchen.

"She's gone," she said. "On her dignity with me to the last, she was, and never once looked at the master when he handed her her wages, and never a word did she say but swept down the steps with never a backward glance."

Adam was filling his cigarette case from a box on the mantel-piece when she went back to the library. The firelight playing across his face revealed the deep lines of those barren years of self-discipline, but there was release, too, in his face, and a younger, softer quality that had not been there before.

"Where will she go, Adam?" she asked him.

"Simmy? She had friends in Plymouth. I've sent a note to Arthur Benyon asking him to give her the once-over. She's not far off a nervous breakdown, I should say, by the look of her."

"Will she—will she be properly cared for?"

"I neither know nor care," he replied. "But Arthur will arrange something."

"Yes, Mr. Benyon is a kind man."

"And I am not, you mean? Well, do you think she deserves much kindness?"

"Yes," said Miranda simply. "Sick minds are not respon-sible, as you should know, Adam."

He smiled a little grimly.

"I'm afraid your opinion of me as a physician is no better than your opinion of me as a husband," he said, and slipped the full case of cigarettes into his breast pocket. "I'm going to see Nanny right away. She, too, has kindness of heart and if she can forgive my injustice sufficiently, I hope to bring her back with me."

"She will come—she said she would," said Miranda. "But would it not do tomorrow?"

"I'm afraid not," he said. "I must," he finished almost shyly, "make my peace with Nanny before I sleep tonight."

She smiled her understanding.

"You will not need to," she said. "Nanny bears no grudge. Shall I come with you, Adam?"

"No, you look tired, and no wonder. Besides, it's easier to humble oneself alone, don't you think?"

She gave a ghost of her provocative laugh as she said, "I cannot see you humble, Adam."

He took her suddenly by the shoulders.

"Can't you?" he said, and his eyes were tender. "You'd find me very humble if you'd try, Miranda."

He kissed her gently and went out of the room.

Miranda listened for the sound of the small car driving away, then went to find Fay.

"Can we go out, Miranda?" the child asked, dancing up and down excitedly. "Can we go to Shap Tor and play hide-and-seek?"

"It's not a very nice day for hide-and-seek," Miranda smiled.

"It isn't bad, now. I want to look for the little shiny stones that Simmy said you can have polished and made into beads. She was going to let me go there by myself this very afternoon, to look for them as a surprise, but I would rather you came, too."

"Simmy was going to let you go alone? Oh, no, Fay, she would not have permitted that," replied Miranda, amused at such a transparent move to persuade her.

"She did say so. She doesn't like the quarry herself but she told me just where to look for the stones. They were to be a surprise for you."

"We will go another day," Miranda said. "But you may play in the garden if you wish, *chérie*. Find a surprise for me there."

"All right," said Fay obligingly. "I will find a lovely surprise for you and then I shall hide it somewhere in the house and you will have to find it."

When the child had left the house Miranda went back to the library and curled up in a big chair by the fire. With the release from strain, lassitude began to claim her limbs and mind.

She awoke to twilight and the sound of the telephone ringing in Adam's study. As she went to answer it, she wondered if it might be Adam calling to say the fog would delay him. But it was Simmy's voice that came to her so unexpectedly over the phone, and the chill of the unheated room made her suddenly shiver.

"Are you alone, Mrs. Chantry?" the voice asked.

"Yes," Miranda replied, puzzled. "My husband is out. Did you wish to speak to him?"

"He's out, is he?" The voice had a pleased note. "No, I didn't wish to speak to him—only to you."

"Yes, Simmy? Where are you?"

"Does it matter where I am, now? You've had your way, haven't you? Did Fay go to the quarry after all?"

"The quarry?" Miranda's voice was sharp. "Of course not. Why should you think that?"

"I had promised to take her. Didn't she tell you? I like to keep a promise, you know, Mrs. Chantry—it's been on my mind."

"Simmy—would she go by herself?" she asked urgently.

There was a little pause, then the colorless voice replied, "I told her she could, Mrs. Chantry, but you should watch her, you know. Have you lost her already, as soon as my back is turned?"

Miranda began to shake.

"Of course not. She went in the garden to play, but she must have come in long ago," she said.

"But you don't know for certain." The voice sounded a little amused. "You should really look for her at the quarry, Mrs. Chantry. I told her to go there, you see, and Fay has always obeyed me. But be careful. The quarry can be dangerous, and I wouldn't like to think any harm should come to you, Mrs. Chantry. Goodbye. . . ."

Miranda heard the click of the receiver being returned to its rest as Simmy hung up.

She did not wait to ring the bell but ran quickly to the kitchen.

"Is Miss Fay out here?" she asked Nancy.

"No, ma'am, I haven't seen her since she went outdoors more than an hour ago," the girl said.

"She would not still be in the garden, though—it is nearly dark," said Miranda, and the urgency in her voice made Nancy look at her more closely.

"My, ma'am, you'm looking quite mazed," she exclaimed. "Miss Fay's in the schoolroom, like as not. Will I go and give her a call for you?"

"No, I'll go."

But there was no sign of the child in the schoolroom or anywhere else. Miranda stood on the stairs and shouted, then ran out into the garden and shouted again.

Nancy came to meet her from the back of the house.

"Her's not outdoors, ma'am," she said. "Be 'ee sure her's not in the house?"

"She's gone to Shap Tor—to the quarry," Miranda said, and Nancy drew her back into the warmth of the house.

"Oh, now ma'am, her'd never go there alone. Why, she was always asking, but Miss Simms had a dislike of the place."

Miranda began to explain, a little incoherently, about Simmy's telephone call. As she listened, Nancy's eyes grew round and some of Miranda's own alarm was written in her pleasant country face.

"What'll us do?" she asked.

Miranda replied, "I must go and find her. At least, if I stand and shout from the road she will hear me and not be frightened."

"Then I'll come with you," the girl said, "I'll just tell Mrs. Yeo, and—"

"No," said Miranda, "she will delay me, and it is better you stay and explain to Mr. Chantry when he returns. I will be quite safe, Nancy, but I must find the poor little girl, and whoever returns first can come for us. Now, quickly—get me a flashlight, if you please."

She set forth in the clammy mist. Over the old clapper bridge and fork left at the crossroads, she remembered, and then it was straight forward down the hill and up the other side to the familiar rocks and boulders of Shap Tor. But the fog was tricky. One moment a patch would clear and the next a wall of mist would cut off all vision for a few brief yards. But as she breasted the last rise to the tor, the mist seemed to clear a little and the sky behind Shap Tor lightened with the first hint of moonrise.

Miranda began to call, but her voice sounded small and lonely in the darkness, and there was no reply. She reached the old quarry, and once she heard an answer to her shout—a noise that might have been a child or only a curlew crying from the bog. The battery of her flashlight was growing weak, but the dim light showed an old track leading into the quarry, and she took it, calling as she went, stumbling over the rough ground. The silence and the darkness of the moor closed in behind her.

The flashlight had to be conserved now for the homeward journey, and she switched it off, feeling with her hands for obstructions and pausing every so often to shout again. She called again, and her voice came back to her in a perfect echo. She took another step forward and stopped suddenly, frozen by a nameless dread. There was nothing to make her hesitate save perhaps an added chill in the air and the sound of water that seemed to be under her feet. But as she switched on the flashlight she saw for a moment the yawning chasm at her feet, the broken platform on which she stood and the gleam of water far below. The light slipped from her hand and fell, echoing strangely in the darkness until at last it reached the bottom of the old mine shaft.

Miranda stood trembling on the brink and covered her face with her hands. Now she knew why Simmy had never liked the quarry. It was here, here at this very spot that Melisande had leaped or fallen to her death, and she, with one more step, would have gone the same way.

It seemed to her an eternity while she stood not daring to move, listening to the dripping water. But it was not, in reality, long afterward that she heard voices shouting, Adam's and Bidder's, so close that the road could not be far away.

She shouted back to them and heard Adam's voice, sharp with anxiety, call, "Miranda! Are you all right?"

"Yes," she replied, and heard the tremble in her own voice. "But I dare not move without a light. I am on the edge of the old mine shaft."

"God!" she heard him exclaim, and almost at once a light shone down on her and she could see him, silhouetted against the sky for one moment before he started down the little path that she had been unable to see.

"Stand quite still," he said quietly. "There's no danger, but those boards won't stand my weight. Give me your hand when I tell you and I'll pull you up."

It was all very quick and simple. She felt his firm hand grip hers and in a moment he had pulled her onto the path beside him and his arms were around her, holding her close in blessed safety.

"Fay . . ." she said, half crying against his breast. "I have not found her, Adam. . . ."

"She's safe at home," he told her with the roughness of intense relief. "She was never out of the house except for a short time in the garden."

"But I do not understand. I called and called and so did Nancy," she said, bewildered.

"She heard you calling, but she was in a cupboard hiding a surprise for you and didn't want to give it away."

She began to laugh a little wildly and he gave her cheek a sharp slap.

"It's nothing to be amused about," he said harshly. "What possessed you to rush off like that and give me the worst half hour I've ever spent in my life? You might have guessed it was only you that crazy woman wanted to frighten. Now, let's get out of this damnable place."

She followed him in silence back to the road, but in the car, Adam drew her against his breast in the darkness and she felt, with surprise, his strong hands tremble as they touched her face.

"Sorry I had to be rough with you," he said. "You'd had a shock."

He did not speak anymore, but held her hard against him while the car made the short journey home, and it was Nanny Coker who took her away from Adam as soon as they reached the house.

"A tray?" Miranda said with disgust as Nanny told her that dining downstairs was forbidden tonight. "But I am not ill, Nanny."

"That's as maybe, m'dear, but master says a tray upstairs and keep warm by the fire. He'll be up later to give you an overhaul."

Miranda grimaced.

"He has the most clinical of minds, even at moments like this, that one," she said, and Nanny's eyes twinkled suddenly.

"There's no telling but what he doesn't need time to pull himself together," she said. "You'm not the only one to be upset today, let me tell you, Miss Miranda, and my advice to you is allow a gentleman to court you in his own fashion however daft it may seem."

Miranda laughed.

"And you think a stethoscope and thermometer are signs of tender devotion?" she asked.

"Well," replied Nanny, not to be daunted, "I don't doubt but the poor gentleman is out of practice."

Nanny lingered while Miranda put on a long velvet housecoat in which to partake of her solitary dinner, and while she sat brushing her hair Nanny chatted of her plans for Fay.

"School later on to rub the corners off and in the meantime the child must get to know her father. . . . We'll soon have her out of that nasty schoolroom and move her to somewhere brighter—the old nursery, perhaps, until it's needed again. . . ."

"It may never be needed, Nanny," said Miranda quietly. But Ellen Coker took no notice of this remark and went straight on with her own conversation while she drew a low table up to the fire in readiness for Miranda's supper and placed a chair in position.

"Nanny—has he changed much?" Miranda asked suddenly.

Nanny straightened her back and looked into the fire.

"Well, yes, m'dear—he's older, of course, but he shouldn't look the way he does with a young bride to make him young again."

"He works too hard," Miranda said. "Was he—was he always so—professional—so hard to know?"

Nanny Coker came and stood behind her, looking into the young, troubled eyes reflected in the glass.

"What are you trying to ask me, m'dear?" she said.

Miranda sighed.

"I do not quite know. You see, he makes me feel that to be young is—not enough. I cannot catch up with him."

"Too old for you, is he, like they all say?" said Nanny calmly, and Miranda turned swiftly from the mirror to catch at her hands.

"No, no—it is I who am too young, and so he will not see me as I am," she cried.

"Then," said Nanny reasonably, "you must make un." She smiled suddenly, her soft skin puckering into many tiny wrinkles. "He isn't as blind as you make out, m'dear, but he's got a lot of daft notions like the gentry sometimes get and call it chivalry or some such highfalutin name. Fair mazed with fear he was when he heard where you'd gone this evening. Didn't he thank the good God you were safe when he found you?"

"No, he slapped me," said Miranda, and Ellen Coker gave a broad smile.

"And so I should hope leading 'ee a dance like that!" she retorted. "As if his hair wasn't gray enough already without you adding to it! Now, here's Nancy with your supper tray and you eat every bit of it or it wouldn't surprise me if you don't get slapped again."

ADAM CAME UPSTAIRS soon after Nancy had cleared away the supper things.

"How do you feel now?" he asked.

"Very well," she replied sedately. "Have you a stethoscope in your pocket?"

He smiled.

"Yes, Nanny warned me that you might not care for a consulting-room manner," he said imperturbably. "However, you will have to humor my peculiarity later on, I'm afraid. I like to keep an eye on that heart of yours."

"My heart," she said a little plaintively, "needs other treatment, I think. Your stethoscope is not infallible."

His eyebrows rose.

"Indeed? You will have to enlarge my medical knowledge for me, then. My stethoscope has been my only guide so far."

She looked at him under her lashes and was all at once rather shy of him. Was he, she wondered with surprise, flirting with her a little in his dry, deceptive fashion? But the next moment he added, with gentle mockery, "It's not very romantic to be married to a surgeon, is it, Miranda?"

"But I have told you, Adam, I am not at all romantic."

"Aren't you? What a pity."

She gave him a startled glance.

"But that is what you liked to hear," she said.

His voice was suitably grave as he replied, "Quite correct. You do well to remind me."

They sat by the fire in a fitful silence while they drank their coffee.

"Did Nanny take much persuading to come back?" she asked, to break the silence.

"No," he replied, setting down his empty cup. "As you said, she bore no grudge, the remarkable woman. Also, she seemed to think she was needed here for your sake as much as Fay's."

"For me?"

"She told me you needed looking after properly. She seems to have taken a fancy to you."

"Oh!"

"Don't I look after you properly, Miranda?"

She met his eyes gravely.

"But you are of the most attentive, always," she replied. "Examinations, thermometers—"

"And stethoscopes—I know, but I don't think that's quite what Nanny meant."

He took the empty cup from her and then moved the coffee tray to another part of the room.

"I think, Miranda," he said quietly, "you and I had better have a little talk."

He came and stood with his back to the fire, looking down at her. All at once she found it difficult to meet his eyes.

"Yes, Adam," she said in a small voice.

"Don't you think we ought to straighten out this marriage of ours once and for all?"

Dismay touched her. She remembered that other night, when he had been on the point of offering her back her freedom. Had he, she wondered, become fond enough of her to have acquired the chivalrous notions that Nanny had said the gentry were prone to, or did he perhaps feel now that his child's affection might be given back to him, his hasty marriage was no longer necessary?

Watching her, he misunderstood the dismay in her eyes and said a little grimly, "You don't find me such an ogre, do you, my dear?"

"Oh, no, no!" she said quickly.

"Well, I'm glad to hear it, because the time has come when I think we should make the best of things, and put our marriage on a normal basis."

She did not answer and he went on, examining his well-kept hands with careful attention.

"I'm fully aware that the terms of our bargain didn't include a—closer relationship between us, but I had an idea at one time that such a relationship wouldn't have been altogether distasteful to you. I—circumstances that I should have had the sense to ignore caused me to handle the situation badly and for that I apologize and also for my attitude toward young Morel."

He stopped speaking abruptly and seemed to be waiting for her to reply, but she felt helpless in the face of such an academic diagnosis. Did he want her, she thought unhappily, or was he in his stiff fashion offering amends for his inability to love her?

She left her chair by the fire and went and stood by one of the windows with her back to him and drew back the curtains. It was a lovely night.

Adam said, a little sadly, "Have I misunderstood you too greatly to retrieve anything from this sorry business?"

"No," she said from the window. "I did not expect understanding from you, Adam. You had so many problems and—Wintersbride is not a very happy house, I think."

"You've never liked it, have you?"

"It's a sad name."

"And an appropriate name for you, you're thinking? Yes, my dear, I'm afraid you're right. I'm too old for you. Is it your freedom that you really want, Miranda?"

She still did not turn from the window, and he thought there were tears in her voice as she said, "You do not understand anything at all. Please put out the light, Adam. I will have more courage in the dark to say the things I must."

He switched off all the lights, but the room was not in darkness. Firelight flickered warmly on the walls and ceiling, and by the window Miranda stood in a patch of moonlight, looking very small and alone.

Adam came and stood behind her, drawing her head back gently against him.

"You don't need courage to tell me the truth," he said. "I will understand, you know, if, after all, you cannot give me what I want. Believe me I only desire your happiness—whatever way that may lie."

"Oh, you are so stupid—so very, very stupid!" she cried and turned suddenly into his arms in a storm of tears.

"Darling, don't . . ." he said, his face twisted with concern. "I know I'm stupid over these matters, but you have only to tell me what you want. . . . Tell me, for heaven's sake, and even if it means releasing you from our crazy contract, I'll do it. . . . Only don't wring my heart like this."

For the first time she was aware of the pain in his voice and of the warmth and protection that at last flowed from him unchecked. Her hands groped blindly for his shoulders and met and clasped tightly behind his neck.

"Adam . . . I cannot any longer pretend . . ." she wept, "I am not p-practical as I told you . . . I am romantic, *hélas*, and I will not mind the house or anything if only you will let me love you a little. . . . I do not even care anymore that perhaps you cannot love me, and if what you were offering is only because you are a man and I to you am at last a woman, I do not mind that, either, if you will let me love you. . . ."

He looked down at her bowed head upon his breast, and gathered her closer against him.

"But what are you telling me, child?" he demanded harshly. "I never for a moment imagined, or even hoped—Miranda, are you trying to tell me that you love me?"

She lifted her face then, and her eyes, unable any longer to hide what was in her heart, looked into his.

"But of course," she said. "I could not help it, after all, and I am afraid I do not care any longer if you should be embarrassed, Adam."

His mouth closed on hers, tenderly at first, then with increasing urgency, and he picked her up and carried her back to the fire.

She leaned against him, a little shaken, and said, rubbing the tears from her lashes, "Then you are not embarrassed, Adam?"

He laughed and put a hand under her chin, lifting her face to his again.

"My darling child, what do you think I've been trying to tell you all evening?" he asked with tender humor. "Did you think I had only a professional interest in setting our affairs right?"

"You did not put your case very well," she said. "Nanny perhaps was right. She said you would be out of practice."

He suddenly knelt beside her in the firelight and took her face between his hands.

"Miranda—I told you that you would find me humble if you would only try," he said. "I feel very humble now, my darling, for I don't think I've yet made you understand how much I love you."

"But yes," she replied with a little smile. "For I do not think you would kiss me like that just to please me." The firelight sparkled on his frosty hair and she drew his head against her breast. . . .

A long time later he said, "And what of Wintersbride, Miranda? Shall we get rid of the place and start afresh, or shall we keep it and—allow the name to be salutary lesson for us both?"

Miranda rested against his shoulder, her eyes already heavy with sleep, and considered. Wintersbride, with its blind shutters, its air of secrecy and its sad link with the past . . . could it ever be home? Yet home was where the heart was, so Nanny would tell her, and had not a house a right to happiness, too?

She turned her head more comfortably into the crook of Adam's shoulder and reached up a hand to touch his face.

"Let us keep it," she said sleepily. "It has a nursery that will be most convenient."